Dark Chapters: Noah

The Oncoming Storm

G000042561

Andrew R Guyatt

© Andrew R Guyatt 2011
First published 2001 as Noah (Cromwell Publishers/First Century) and 2006
as The Day the Sky Opened (Scripture Union)
The Oncoming Storm is an adaptation of *The Day the Sky Opened*.
ISBN 978 1 84427 619 6

Scripture Union
207–209 Queensway, Bletchley, Milton Keynes, MK2 2EB
Email: info@scriptureunion.org.uk
Website: www.scriptureunion.org.uk

Scripture Union Australia
Locked Bag 2, Central Coast Business Centre, NSW 2252
Website: www.scriptureunion.org.au

Scripture Union USA
PO Box 987, Valley Forge, PA 19482
Website: www.scriptureunion.org

British Library Cataloguing-in-Publication Data
A catalogue record of this book is available from the British Library.

Printed and bound in India by Nutech Print Services

Cover design: GoBallistic

Scripture Union is an international charity working with churches in more
than 130 countries, providing resources to bring the good news of Jesus Christ
to children, young people and families and to encourage them to develop
spiritually through the Bible and prayer.

As well as our network of volunteers, staff and associates who run holidays,
church-based events and school Christian groups, we produce a wide range
of publications and support those who use our resources through training
programmes.

1

He was near the river by the altar where they burned babies to the gods. But the ash and blood had gone, scoured by the torrential rain beating on the stones. He was alone, soaked to the skin and terrified. Choking mist and water hammered down in a never-ending torrent.

Above the din of the storm there was a new noise: a distant rumble like thunder in the hills. It grew nearer and nearer. Desperately, he forced himself to turn and face it. Through the gloom came a great wave of water higher than the tower of the temple.

There was nowhere to run. The last thing he saw was the foaming edge of the wave curling over, with huge trees floating on it like leaves. Then it was on him, smashing him against the altar.

It was dawn and the haunting nightmare – that thing he could never bring himself to talk about – was slowly fading. He was in his room, sprawled on the floor beside his pallet. His throat felt sore from screaming.

Through a gap in the shutter he saw the hills turning gold as the sun rose, bone dry as they always were in late summer. No mist, no driving rain or waves; just the old familiar world.

A noise distracted him. Zillah had woken.

'Noah! What is it?'

'I'm sorry. It's…'

'That dream again? The one you keep getting?'

He nodded, wiping his forehead. It was cool in the room, but he was rank with sweat.

'I'm so scared! Something terrible's going to happen! Tiamat is trying to warn you.'

'Tiamat – that chaos monster of yours – it doesn't exist!'

'So who sends the big wave, then?'

'What? I've never told you about that!'

'You don't have to. You keep screaming that the water's coming to swallow you. The servants think you've been cursed and if they leave we'll have no one to protect us from the Cainites.'

'But what can I do?'

'You might make a sacrifice to Marduk. He's the one god strong enough to deal with Tiamat.'

'I'll never worship that demon!'

'Look, all I'm suggesting is one small sacrifice. No one will think less of you.'

'No!'

'But we can't go on like this.'

Noah paused. 'I wonder if I should go and see the old ones.'

'Run to your daddy and grandpa for them to kiss you better? They'll stuff your head with old-fashioned ideas'

'But I need to talk it over with them.'

'What about me? I'm scared when you go away! They say the Cainites are on the march again.'

'I'll be as quick as I can. I'll leave my foreman Reu with you. He won't stand any nonsense.'

'Love, do you have to go?'

'Yes, I want to sacrifice to the Holy One.'

'You and your Holy One! If he's that special why doesn't anyone else worship him? Just you and your doddering family!'

There was a painful silence.

'I'm sorry, Noah. I shouldn't have said that... but if you must go, take Tiras – and lose him!'

'What's he been up to?'

'The usual! That stupid granddaughter of Eber is having his brat! Get him out of my hair!'

He took ten men – loyal, experienced fighters who would keep their eyes open and their weapons within reach. Each had a bow and arrows, a spear with a fire-hardened tip and a flint dagger. They took food for a week, presents for the old ones and a lamb for the sacrifice.

His assistant foreman Seth roused him before dawn and they left quietly to avoid waking the household, but Zillah was there to wave him goodbye and tell him to look after himself.

The sun rose as they reached the road running from the city to the mountains. They walked silently, alert to any signs of danger. Then Seth touched Noah's arm.

'There, Master! Some folk near the road.'

'Keep going. They don't look like Cainites.'

They disappeared into the scrub but Noah looked anxiously after them, conscious of sweat trickling down his neck. Half-expecting a spear in his back, he clutched his dagger until his fingers were stiff.

There were other people too, gathering wood or picking berries. Then they saw several men together. Once more, Noah tensed up, then Seth remarked, 'They must be hunters after deer or a fat bear to grease their stomachs!'

As dusk fell, they reached their usual camping site, a small hill where men had burnt a patch of forest and cultivated the soil until it lost its vigour. The trees had not grown back and there was a clear view all round.

They ate bread and cheese, stretching out tired legs towards the fire. Then the men took turns keeping watch. Seth slept little since he kept checking the lookouts but he still managed to wake Noah at first light.

'Master, it feels like winter's coming. I'll be glad to sleep indoors tonight!'

The path steepened and their pace slowed. Beech and oak trees gave way to pine and birch and the track narrowed as they left the main settlements behind. It was much colder here and the men stuffed their sandals with hay and put on cloaks of woven grass. Then suddenly they emerged onto bleak moorland, blinking in the late afternoon sun and shivering in the bitter wind.

Ahead was a long low building sheltered in a fold of the hill, with a tower at one end, stark against the sky, a lonely place at the edge of the world. As they hurried up the hill there was a shout.

'Do you come in peace?'

'Yes!' Seth bellowed. 'It's Noah and his men. Let us in, it's cold out here!'

The gate creaked open and they walked in.

'Welcome, Noah! This is a very pleasant surprise.'

It was his father Lamech, with grandfather Methuselah hobbling out of a doorway behind him. They were wizened old men, more like brothers than father and son, dried out like fruit left in a store, but their eyes darted everywhere, missing nothing.

'You must pardon us. If we had known you were coming we would have had a meal prepared.'

Lamech clapped his hands. 'Adam! Food for my son and his men! They are frozen after their journey.'

Soon Noah was reclining in front of a blazing fire, and Adam, a bent old man looking as ancient as his namesake, brought him a cup of milk.

'It's good to see you again, Master. The women are preparing your meal.'

There was gruel, cheese and butter made from sheep's milk, rough bread and, as a treat, berries sweetened with honey. But although Noah ate well, the old ones merely pecked at their food, impatient to learn the reason for his visit.

After they had finished, his father asked after the family, then Methuselah spoke.

'Noah, do you want to tell us something?'

'Well, sir... there is a dream I keep having.'

Lamech interrupted. 'Speak up. Your grandfather and I can hardly hear you.'

Noah began talking slowly and loudly, but even as he described his nightmare it sounded thin and unreal. However, Methuselah looked very interested.

'My son, I believe the Holy One has spoken to you, just as he did to my father Enoch.'

And he began retelling a familiar story.

'I used to sit on my father's knee while he told me what my ancestors were called and how long they had lived. He said that every name had a meaning. His meant "to start a work".'

He chuckled and reached for his cup.

'Then I asked him why I was called Methuselah. He said the Holy One had suggested this to him in a dream while my mother was carrying me.'

As a child, Noah had always prompted him at this point, and again he asked the old question.

'Sir, what did it mean?'

'It is a prophecy: "after he dies it will be sent". When I depart, the Holy One will bring a terrible judgement on men for their wickedness. But while I am still here, there is time to repent.'

'But, sir, they are just as evil as ever!'

'Indeed! In a few years I will go to my rest and I tremble to think what will happen then. Nobody, not even my dear father, knew what this judgement would be, but I believe it is revealed in your dream. The Holy One has chosen you to stand in this evil time, and if you are faithful he will reveal more. It will not be easy, but your father and I are here to help. Tomorrow we will sacrifice to the Holy One and seek his will.'

2

That night he dreamed he was in the Garden of Eden. It was bursting with life, the trees weighed down with flowers and fruit, their colours brighter than any he knew. A gazelle lifted its head to be stroked, a bear growled contentedly as he scratched its shoulder and sheep mixed fearlessly with lions.

The man and woman were wrapped in light, the most joyous couple he had ever seen. He was digging; then he took a young shoot and tenderly planted it. She was cuddling chicks while the hen clucked contentedly nearby. They looked like children playing, but then Noah realised that in a few minutes they had achieved more than he could in a whole day.

Then the sun was sinking and the garden gate opened. Noah was half-blinded by glory, but glimpsed the couple running to the Holy One and swinging on his arms.

How he wished this would never end, but all too soon he saw the evil one, shining and covered in gold and jewels. He had once been the chief angel, but then he had lusted for more power and the Holy One had hurled him out of heaven.

The woman knew nothing of this. She was dazzled by his beauty and he deceived her so very quickly: first a doubt, then a lie and finally a desire for forbidden knowledge. In a moment she had picked, tasted and shared the fruit. As he watched, the aura of light around the couple faded and, suddenly embarrassed, they grabbed for fig leaves to cover their nakedness. Then they hid.

That evening the Holy One returned. He stripped the evil one of his ornaments, leaving him as a humble snake, foretold that the woman would have agony when she bore children and transformed the man's joyful work into backbreaking toil. They were expelled from the garden to die outside, and the gate was shut and guarded by cherubim with flaming swords. The Holy One was left alone, weeping for the friends he had banished.

But somehow the couple found courage to start again. Eve had two sons, while Adam grew crops and tamed sheep. But then their son Abel was murdered by his brother Cain, who as a result was banished. Noah recoiled as he saw his bitter face, a man too proud to ask for forgiveness, a dreadful example for his children.

Then he saw Lamech the Cainite genius, teaching his three sons. Jabal learned to tame wild cattle, Jubal became a musician, a maker of harps and pipes, and Tubal-Cain began to forge bronze and iron. But Lamech was also violent and vengeful, boasting of killing a boy who had merely struck him.

Then Noah entered their temple. There was the thudding of drums and wailing of horns and despite the darkness he saw masked dancers. They were maddened by drugs, and on the altar a baby's body still twitched. For a moment he stared, unwilling to believe what he was seeing, then he rubbed his eyes as if he could somehow wipe out the horror of what he had experienced.

Now he saw his ancestor Seth, Adam's third son. There was hope, men were calling on the Holy One, but soon they fell under the Cainite spell. Men became evil, degrading everything and everyone. Worst of all were the Nephilim: huge men, the sons of demons who had seduced women. Their eyes probed him as if they would rip out his soul.

Now he was outside the temple where his great-grandfather Enoch was prophesying to the crowd.

'You are defying the Holy One! But he's coming to judge you!'

The mob was furious. Some spat in his face, others threw stones and one man hurled a clod of dung into his face. Then someone shouted, 'If your god's any good, why doesn't anyone else worship him?'

But Enoch continued, 'You won't escape; the Holy One's coming with an army of hundreds of thousands who love him. They'll judge you for every filthy thing you've done.'

They surged forward but somehow he faced them down and there was silence as he strode away.

Noah woke in the dark, moaning, 'Zillah's right! No one believes in the Holy One now!'

But soon he was asleep again. He was in the Great Valley; it was autumn and a mass of black cloud was spilling over the western hills; there would be a terrible storm.

'I must escape to the hills,' he cried, but it was too late. The rain blinded him and in an awful moment he knew that this was turning into his terrible nightmare and soon the wave would smash him against the altar.

Instead he watched as the rain clouds swept in; earthquakes released underground springs and the sea surged over the land. People waded then swam or clutched pieces of wood until the torrents overcame them. Soon he could only see water.

'Holy One, that's horrible! Horrible! It can't happen!'

Then doubts seeped into his mind. 'Perhaps Tiamat is doing this, or is this the Holy One enjoying his revenge?'

Immediately he felt ashamed as he sensed God's grief. 'No, this is all our fault! We've fouled up his beautiful world and he can't find anything worth keeping!'

Then he saw the flood again, but now something was floating in the water. It was huge, more like a box or ark than a boat, and covered with a thatched roof. Inside were two floors of stores and above a deck with every kind of animal and bird: oxen, sheep, doves and pigeons and also wolves, vultures, lions and biting insects.

He saw Zillah tending them, although now her hair was white, and those men with her must be his sons grown up and those women their wives. But who was this stooped old man?

'Oh no! I hope I never look that decrepit!' he exclaimed.

Now the ark had landed on dry land and the people and animals emerged. The ruined world had been restored and they had another chance.

But where could he find·this ark?

Then he saw scaffolding down by the river, and he was supervising some men as they rolled great tree trunks into position.

'Holy One! Not me! I can't build it! I'm just a farmer. And I'm too old, I want to retire, it would take years – far longer than I've got left. Zillah and the neighbours would think I'd gone mad. How could I pay for it and where would I get the wood?'

Once more he slept. Now he saw a dark sea, but these were ancient waters and the Spirit of the Holy One was watching over them. Then everything burst into existence, light and darkness, sky, sea and land, and the sun, moon and stars singing for joy. It teemed with plants and animals and he saw the Holy One breathing life into the man.

Then he knew the Spirit was breathing into him too. He had received power to make this thing.

3

As a boy Noah wondered why they did not live in the Great Valley. Then one day Methuselah explained.

'We had a fine house by the river and were respected by our neighbours although we did not worship their gods. But after Enoch prophesied against them they became very angry and we had to move. So we came here, well away from the idols and wickedness.'

'It's a lovely spot!'

'You should have seen it when we arrived! Your dear grandmother wept because it was so cold. Beyond those mountains was a valley filled with ice and snow.'

'I want to see that!'

'Maybe, but many men believed that ice demons lived there which feasted on human flesh. And on winter nights when the wind howled our servants would huddle together chanting spells against them.'

'Have you seen an ice demon, Grandfather?'

'No! That's a silly story invented by those who do not know the Holy One. Some day I will take you to that valley to show you that it is safe.'

'Is there still snow there?'

'Only grass and pools of water.'

'Will the ice come back?'

'I hope not! It is warmer now and we can grow more crops. When you were born we called you Noah, or "comfort", since we believed the Holy One was comforting us and helping us raise crops from the land he had cursed. We feel blessed to have such a faithful son who will make this place a refuge for true worshippers.'

But Noah was desperate to explore the outside world and bombarded the servants with questions. One autumn day he spoke to Lamech.

'Why don't we move back to the Great Valley? The ground here's poor; we'd do better by the river.'

'How dare you! Never let me hear you say that again! The Holy One gave us this home safe from idolaters and those who would harm us. All you want is a full belly and slave girls!'

Noah was taken aback by his father's ferocity. 'But there's no harm in having a look...'

'Look? Once you get among those dreadful people you will be serving their gods before you can turn around and...'

He raged on while his son stood silent. But Noah still longed to go there, and whenever the weather permitted he would climb the hill to look down over the forbidden land.

Then one spring evening, to his surprise, Lamech brought the subject up again.

'Do you still want to go down into the valley?'

'Well... yes, Father. But only with your blessing.'

'We had such hopes for you, my son, that you would worship the Holy One when we were gone. But now you want to throw all it all away.'

'No, Father! I simply want to see what it's like down there.'

'I am afraid that evil influences are drawing you away.'

'No, I think the Holy One himself is telling me to go!'

Next day they spoke again.

'Your grandfather and I were discussing your future late into the night. We have decided that you may go down into the Great Valley – but you only have until autumn to prove yourself. Otherwise you must come straight back here. We will be calling on the Holy One for your safety.'

A few days later, Noah set off. A distant relative rented him some land near the river and he planted wheat. He had a bumper crop, which paid off his debt and left him with several sacks to take home.

His family were amazed by the change in him; the slender boy had broadened into a man with firm muscles and a confident air.

'I never believed I would say this,' Lamech confided, 'but your time in the Great Valley has done you good. That is as long as you have avoided idolatry and still worship the Holy One.'

Soon Noah settled there permanently and his farm prospered. Despite the fears of the old ones, he kept his faith and even persuaded them to visit him.

They were amazed by his herd of cattle.

'I bred them from a bull and cows I bought from the Cainites,' he explained.

'How did you manage that?' Lamech asked.

'I don't know. Perhaps I caught them by surprise. Nowadays they neuter every male they sell, so my neighbours come to me to have their cows served.'

The old ones gaped when they saw how much milk each cow produced and admired the oxen ploughing the fields and also the donkeys.

'These are what you need in the hills,' Noah explained. 'They're more nimble than oxen and you can even ride them.'

But Lamech was impressed most of all by Noah's men.

'They work very cheerfully and well, my son. You are fortunate.'

'That's due to your example. I copied the way you look after your own servants, feeding them well and treating them like free men. They're my eyes and ears; no one steals from me and I get little trouble from my neighbours.'

'Do your men worship the Holy One?'

'I fear not, but they respect my beliefs.'

The old ones took several donkeys with them when they left. They promised to return, but the years had passed and they became too frail for the journey.

Then Noah married Zillah, the daughter of a local farmer. Her family home was full of idols but she agreed to worship the Holy One. She objected, however, to her new house.

'Do we have to live in this shack?'

'No, dear, once harvest is over, I'll build you the best house in the Great Valley!'

And he did. His settlement had a watchtower, granaries and sheds for the cattle, but the centrepiece was a farmhouse with five separate rooms, a wonder to his neighbours who were crammed into huts.

He bought more land, expanding his farm into an estate until he became one of the richest men in the Great Valley. He never had a bad harvest and was always looking for more space for his grain and animals.

Then, after years of waiting, he had three sons. The oldest was Shem, meaning "name", to remind him of the name of the Holy One, then came Japheth, or "expand" – a tribute to how the Holy One had blessed him materially. The youngest was Ham, or "hot" – a name that fitted him perfectly.

Now they were growing up and soon would have their own wives and families.

'Maybe,' he suggested to Zillah, 'I can pass some of my responsibilities over to them. I'm not as young as I used to be and I'm tired of pushing myself. It would give us more time together.'

But that very night his nightmares started, and now he had a new, enormous task.

That evening he had a final look around.

'The homestead looks good for a thousand years, but if my dream is true it'll vanish soon!'

Then he stared at the buildings, fixing every detail in his mind.

After supper he told the old ones of his latest dream.

Methuselah nodded. 'I thank the Holy One for giving you this vision. He will keep his promise to you, as he did to my father Enoch.'

Noah left next morning as the first rays of the sun lit the watchtower. The old ones hobbled to the gate to see him go and he had a strong urge to stay and share their final days. But there was work to do and he went, wondering if he would see them again.

Soon they left the sunlit moor and plunged into the misty forest. Then he began to have doubts.

'Are things really that bad? The Cainites do horrible things, and it is not much better in the city, but my neighbours are good folk. I'm only sorry they don't worship the Holy One.'

Then Seth signalled for silence, cupping his hand to his ear.

'Do you hear that, Master?'

Noah noticed a strange pulsation, first a vibration in his belly, then a noise assailing him from all directions.

'It sounds like a drum.'

Seth nodded grimly. 'Before we go on, let's check what's out there.'

He and Tiras hurried forward while the others waited apprehensively. Then he reappeared, running hard, struggling to catch his breath.

'Master... bad trouble... bodies... killers can't be far...'

Noah glanced around nervously. This was the ideal place for an ambush: a narrow path hemmed in by woodland.

The drumming had stopped, so Noah gave an order.

'Let's go! There's a clearing ahead where we can defend ourselves.'

But when they reached the open space they found two human torsos. Their heads and legs were missing and their chests gaped open.

Seth pointed. 'Whoever did that wanted their hearts. They say if you eat them it gives you the spirit of the man you've killed. They've also taken the legs; there's good meat on them!'

Noah was horrified. 'Cannibals? I thought that was only a story to frighten naughty children?'

'Here's the fire and there are the leg bones, cracked open to get the marrow. Those are bits of skull. Looks like they roasted the heads whole.'

Noah retched until he thought he would bring his stomach up.

'Let's go, Master. I don't want to get eaten!'

'No, we will bury them first. I won't leave them for the vultures.'

The men were very frightened but he insisted. They dug a shallow grave, lifted in the bodies and bones from the fire, then scraped the soil back.

Noah's doubts had been resolved.

4

Zillah was waiting when they returned. 'Oh, am I glad you're back! I've been really scared.'

'Did anything happen?'

'You may well ask! A gang tried to break in yesterday, and if it hadn't been for Reu, we'd have lost everything. I'm terrified they'll come back!'

This was clearly no time for Noah to tell her of his visions, and the next few days he was busy catching up with his work. But one morning he found her alone. He swallowed and was clearing his throat when she spoke.

'Noah! I know you want to tell me about your wretched nightmares, but I'm not interested!'

'I'm sorry, but it's very important.'

'Can't we leave it? I've got a lot to do.'

'But I've got to tell you sooner or later.'

'All right then, but make it quick.'

She stared at the wall as he tried to explain. Then, embarrassed, he tailed off mid-sentence.

'Is that it? May I go now?'

Had she understood anything? Who else could he discuss this with? How he needed support and advice where to begin!

Of course, he knew about boats. He used them regularly to ferry goods and livestock. He had coracles fashioned out of cowhide, two reed boats and for heavier loads rafts made of tree trunks lashed together.

'But this is gigantic! Who's ever seen a raft with side walls three floors high and a roof?' he wondered.

He fretted all winter, but the Holy One remained silent. Then, one night in spring, he had another vision.

He was drifting down the river; then he heard a voice.

'This is where you must build your ark.'

It was a field just inside the estate boundary, a morning's walk from the settlement. The main road from the city ran close by.

'But this is the worst place! That road is used all the time, and everyone will see what I'm doing. Let's put it in the middle of the estate.'

'Noah, I'm choosing you to warn everyone of the coming judgement. They must see what you're doing.'

'Couldn't we move it just beyond those trees?'

'It must be in full view as a warning of the coming judgement.'

'But any passer-by can steal or vandalise it.'

'I will protect it – and you too.'

Next he was standing on the riverbank and the field had been cleared of trees. Years before, the river had changed course leaving a blind inlet, and this was now full of rafts while oxen dragged heavy loads up the bank.

Nearby was a clay pit where his men were making bricks. They were constructing a huge elongated structure, a series of breast-high brick towers supporting a timber lattice. On top of this, men were lashing baulks of timber together and daubing them with pitch.

Then he understood.

'It's a cradle! We're going to build the ark on top, so we can get at the underside and keep it clear of termites!'

And now he found himself in a cypress grove with trunks towering high above him and he knew he was in a northern forest. Then, through a gap in the trees, he saw a strange mountain with two peaks. He stared, storing its outline in his memory.

He awoke feeling alert. 'I'll look at that site today. Fortunately things are not too busy as it's three months till harvest.'

Leaving Seth guarding the settlement, he took Reu and a party of men. They walked along the riverbank while a raft loaded with supplies floated behind them.

The men enjoyed a break from their usual routine, but Noah felt uneasy. Then, just as they were arriving, he called a halt.

'Reu, do you smell anything?'

The foreman nodded. 'Master, someone's lit a fire just ahead of us.'

'But it's on our land. I haven't ordered it.'

'Leave it to me, Master. I'll take a look.'

He crawled forward, until he glimpsed a clearing near the river. Several shacks were clustered round a fire. Women were washing clothes and children were playing.

A dog came towards him and began barking until one of the women cuffed it and it ran away. Thankfully, he returned safely to Noah.

'You've got squatters on your land, city folk by the smell of them!'

Leaving a guard on the raft, they crawled to the clearing, then stood up and advanced, spears in hand.

Their approach was a complete surprise. A woman screamed as they reached the shacks, then five naked men tumbled out.

'Any more?' Noah yelled. 'Come on, I want to see you!'

A few more appeared while the women were rounded up. The adults formed a line with their children hiding behind them.

Then Noah spoke. 'You've no right to be here! This is my land.'

Somebody belched loudly and they sniggered. But the laughter died as Noah's men moved forward menacingly.

'Get out! And take your rubbish with you.'

One man began to object, but a spear held close to his throat quelled the protest. Soon they were trudging reluctantly towards the city, clutching their possessions. Then an old woman darted back and spat in Noah's face. Reu was about to run her through when Noah intervened.

'Let her be!'

She jabbed a finger at him. 'I curse you by the gods of the river and forest and the sickness that comes at full moon.'

From the corner of his eye he saw his men turning away, frightened by her curse. Then Reu pulled his sleeve.

'Let me kill her!'

'No! I don't want her blood on my hands.' Turning to her, he shouted, 'Get out!'

She cackled. 'Don't get too comfortable, old man. We'll be back and make short work of you and your men!'

5

Clearing up was a foul job; the squatters had been there for months. It was sunset before they had finished, and they had to sleep in the open.

Noah woke at first light. Something had disturbed him, but all he could hear was the wind and the murmur of the river. Pulling his robe about him he walked round the men and found both watchmen asleep.

Then a twig snapped.

He roused Reu, putting a hand over his mouth to stop him crying out. Then they woke the others and told them to pick up their spears.

There was just time to form a defensive ring before they were attacked from all directions. Men fell, their screams cut off by the sickening jolt of spears tearing into living flesh. Inside the ring Noah glimpsed a white figure and lunged at it with his dagger. He hit it so hard that he had trouble removing the blade afterwards. It slumped to the ground writhing.

Then suddenly the enemy melted away. But Reu kept the men at their posts until the sun rose.

They had only lost one man, but several were hurt. Reu had a reputation as a healer and treated the wounds with poultices of dried leaves and herbs. Six of the attackers lay dead, and another was fatally wounded.

Reu offered him water, but he was too weak to swallow and died, calling for his mother.

Then they noticed the body of the person Noah had stabbed. It lay face down, but when Reu turned it over with his foot Noah stared in horrified fascination. It was the woman who had cursed him.

Her face was twisted in fury and the dead eyes stared accusingly. Then he shouted out.

'Why did she come back? I didn't intend her harm. I never meant to kill her!'

While some of the men buried the dead, he took the rest over to the raft. There had been no time to deal with it before.

'Unload this stuff, then you can erect our shelters.'

Noah lay awake a long time that night worrying. 'If the Holy One meant me to build the ark here, why did he let these people settle? And why did we have to kill so many of them?'

But when he woke late next day, the men were already working, grubbing up bushes and felling trees. Their main problem was a lack of tools, with just two bronze axes. The only people who could make them were the Cainites, and they charged what they liked.

However, he did have five flint axes made at the settlement. The best craftsman was old Eber, who generally worked with a mob of children around him listening to his stories. He wore an eye patch, and liked to push it up and grin at them with an empty socket.

'Got a bit of flint in that eye when I was a lad, and it hurt so bad they took it out. Reckon I'm more careful now – that other one's got to see me through!'

He never hurried, but worked far faster than the other men, reckoning to make an axe a day. The only thing that angered him was a bronze tool.

'I've no faith in these newfangled things!' he would say, spitting on the ground.

He kept Noah well supplied with all manner of tools, including wooden saws embedded with flakes of flint. But despite his prejudice, his flint tools were not as good as bronze ones.

All seemed to be going well until the men found a shrine, an altar stone with the figure of a goddess, and they refused to go near it. Worse still, one of the precious bronze axes disappeared. The culprit had laid it down while he got a drink and someone had stolen it.

Reu picked up a spear. 'Shall I kill him, Master?'

The man was terrified. 'Master, I've got a wife and three little ones – they'll starve without me!'

Noah shook his head. 'Let him go. Killing him won't bring that tool back.'

Then a flint axe shattered, and Noah heard mutterings that they were cursed and the goddess would kill them if they continued work in this sacred place. But that evening Reu came to Noah with a suggestion.

'Master, my wife knows all the ancient secrets. If I fetched her, she could make the proper offerings to appease the goddess and let us move her shrine.'

Noah groaned. Encouraging pagan worship was a betrayal of his beliefs. But there seemed no alternative, and he nodded reluctantly.

Two days later the shrine had vanished and the men were working everywhere. Eber made some fresh axes, and soon the site had been cleared. The large timber was saved for constructing the cradle and the brushwood chopped up for fires and charcoal.

Then some men moved onto adjoining land to cut more wood, while others began levelling the site and burning charcoal.

Reu was becoming very puzzled. 'Why do you want so much charcoal, Master?'

'We're going to fire a lot of bricks.'

'But wouldn't it be easier to use sun-dried ones?'

'They wouldn't be strong enough for what I want. We'll be moving a lot of heavy logs over them and they'd crumble if they weren't really hard. Or they'll wash away if it rains.'

'Won't the roof protect them?'

'We're not building a house; we'll be making a lot of towers – about breast high.'

Reu sounded very confused. 'Well, if that's what you want, Master.'

For a moment Noah nearly explained the whole project to him, but then his courage failed. What would this tough, no-nonsense foreman make of his vision?

The work progressed. Gangs of men dug out clay, mixing it with chopped straw to make it pliable, and moulded bricks which were fired in great clamps.

But the harvest was starting, and most of them would be needed in the fields. For a few weeks Noah could turn his thoughts to gathering in crops. But he was still wondering the best way of telling his men what they were doing.

6

When evil men die, they go to the land of pitch where they join souls in torment. Flames burst from black, stinking pools and the sun is blotted out. Birds drop dead from the sky and even scorpions perish.

But there are men – worshippers of the dread gods of fire, sitting like birds of prey, watching the sacred flame until their eyes cloud over. Their skin is as rough as leather and covered in tumours from the boiling tar.

Even the men of the city dread that place. One of their youths witnessed the terrible full moon feast; he had been snatched from his parents and mutilated, but he escaped before he was thrown into a lake of fire. However, his hair was white and he had to be tied up like a dog.

A trader of pitch told Noah this story when he was a boy, and for weeks afterwards he cowered in his bed at night waiting to be snatched.

Once he woke up screaming and Lamech came to him. So he repeated the story.

'That's superstitious nonsense!'

'But it's true! That man knows the family!'

'Hmm... I heard that yarn when I was a child, only then it was a Cainite boy who was snatched. Your great-grandfather Enoch told me he knew the tale too, but that unfortunate youth was a great-grandson of Adam!'

'So isn't it real?'

'Of course not, but your trader wants to keep his business. If people lose their fear of that place they will go there themselves rather than buy from him.'

'So why don't we do that?'

'It is not worth it for the amount we use. And it is time for you to go back to sleep.'

Since he had lived in the Great Valley Noah had bought from the traders too, but now he needed vast amounts to build the cradle and seal the ark. There seemed no option but to go there personally.

When harvest was over, Noah fasted three days, asking the Holy One for help. Then he gathered his men.

Reu was horrified. 'Master! You can't be asking me to go? I've always done what's right by you, but this...'

'What are you worried about?'

'Well, we won't come back. I hate to think what they'll do when they catch us.'

'That's nonsense!'

'The speaker was Pallu, an older man. 'Don't worry, Master. I've dug pitch there many a time. It's a messy old job but there're worse places to be.'

Noah stared at him. 'So you know it?'

'Oh yes, it's on the river, about a week's journey upstream. You dig your pitch, then you pay for each load at a nearby village.'

'Do they take gold?'

'Yes, but you can barter. They can't grow much and are always after grain and oil. But they drive a hard bargain; you can't find pitch elsewhere and they know it. And one other thing: don't get there at full moon!'

After a lot of persuasion, Noah had 18 nervous volunteers lured by an offer of double wages. Reu stayed behind, so Pallu enjoyed his new status as guide and foreman, but by the time they set off many of the volunteers were having second thoughts and he only spurred them into action by threatening to humiliate them in front of their women. On the third night there was a mutiny, and he quelled it by beating the ringleader unconscious and half-drowning him in the river.

However, despite these problems, they kept going and on the eighth morning Pallu shouted.

'Master, see that smoke? It's from the pitch lakes. Reckon we'll arrive around midday.'

As the morning wore on, the men grew quiet and Noah wondered if they would panic and head back down the river. But to his relief they reached the village and tied up. Then a very fat man appeared, wiping his hands on his greasy robe.

'Enkidu's the name. Come for pitch?'

Without waiting for an answer, he continued, 'You look as if you want a lot; most folk don't bring two rafts. And you've got grain to offer, I hear.'

Noah glanced at the rafts. They were completely shrouded.

Enkidu grinned. 'We don't miss much. What's your olive oil like?'

Noah managed to keep the surprise out of his eyes. 'Everything I have is of the highest quality.'

'We've had a lot in recently. All we need for this year. And as a man of your experience will know, all our pitch is already promised. Traders don't take kindly to outsiders butting in.'

Then Pallu caught Noah's eye.

'Don't waste your time, Master. There're plenty of other agents around.'

Noah turned away, but Enkidu, moving surprisingly fast for a man his size, blocked the way.

'Not so fast! May I suggest…'

Then Pallu stepped between them. 'Master, let me handle this.'

It was sunset when he emerged smiling from Enkidu's hut. 'I got what you wanted, Master. We can load both rafts and still have a bit left over.'

As they walked back to the rafts, Noah heard two men muttering. 'No right to be here… shouldn't let outsiders in…'

'Are those men traders?' he asked.

'Yes, Master, but don't lose sleep over them.'

'But what about the fire worshippers?'

'They're ordinary folk too, like Enkidu here, doing quite nicely out of selling pitch. But they do like you to sacrifice to their gods.'

Next morning the men made their offerings to two hideous idols, but Noah walked away in disgust. On his return he noticed the traders again, but this time they had a gang of slaves with them, trudging along dejectedly. However, one man held his head high; presumably his spirit had not been broken.

Noah's men set off along a narrow path covered in sand drifts and patches of oil. Eventually they reached a desolate area with dark pools emitting gouts of flame, and began work. The pitch was solid, requiring the full weight of a man to cut it. Soon everyone was covered in oil and cursing steadily, and one unfortunate sank waist-deep in a hidden pool. Then they hoisted their baskets onto their backs and staggered back down the path, blinded by sweat pouring into their eyes.

Back at the rafts, they emptied the pitch into wooden boxes sealed with clay then took a deep draught of water before stumbling back for another load. After four trips they were exhausted; they rubbed themselves with sand and bathed in the river in a vain attempt to get clean.

Next day, Noah saw the gang of slaves again. Suddenly there was a commotion and the man who had looked defiant slipped. As he desperately tried to keep his balance, he stumbled into a burning pool.

'Help him!' Noah shouted to his master.

'No, he's a trouble maker. We're better off without him.'

By now his rags had caught fire and he was slowly incinerated alive, his cries rising in a crescendo then gradually weakening.

After five exhausting days, they had a full load and the rafts were almost submerged, leaving oily trails in the water. They set off for home with the oxen swimming behind them.

7

Now they began work.

On the basis of his vision, Noah drew a plan on a clay tablet and showed it to Reu.

'The cradle will lie with its long side facing the river.' He pushed a stake into the ground. 'That's one corner.'

Using a marked rope they planted another stake nearly six metres from the first, then another and another until there were 29 in a line.

'Now we need to lay out the ends; each has eight stakes.'

When these were complete they measured out the other side and filled in the centre with a grid of stakes, each nearly six metres apart.

When they had finished, Noah stood looking at them.

'May the Holy One help me! It's a huge job, and we're only just beginning!'

Noah described how to make the brick towers or piers. Each was square with bricks outside and clay in the middle. The foundations were a metre deep and stood one and a half metres high. Reu made measuring rods to check the height and plumb lines to keep them vertical.

'Master, shall we heat the pitch in an earthenware pot to soften it?' he enquired.

Noah laughed. 'Father tried that once. The pot cracked and the whole hut went up in flames. No, I'll bring some bronze bowls from the settlement.'

That night the men sat discussing the project.

'What's it for?'

'No idea – but it'll take ages!'

'I counted well over two hundred stakes! We'll need a mountain of bricks!'

'And the columns are so short; you won't get a roof on top.'

'Is it some religious thing?'

'Maybe. It's about time the old man built a shrine to his god.'

'I think he's mad!'

'Maybe, but he pays good wages!'

As each pair of adjacent piers reached the right height, the men lifted a timber to bridge the gap between them. Then the sides were built up and the top was sealed. But they were soon running out of pitch, so Noah sent Pallu with a party to collect more. Meanwhile he returned to the settlement.

Zillah looked very sour. 'To what do we owe this honour? Would my lord and master care to enter our humble abode and be introduced to his sons?'

'Are you feeling all right?'

'No! You promised me a year ago you would build a room for the boys, but now you're wasting bricks and the men's time on your madcap scheme!'

'Well come along and see what we're doing.'

After some persuasion she arrived and walked around, her lips pursed. Then she came to the fire, where they were melting pitch, and spotted some bronze.

'In the name of Marduk, what are you doing? You've ruined my bronze pans!'

'I was going to tell you—'

'I've searched for them everywhere. They're covered in muck and I'll never get the scorch marks out. It'll cost half our estate to replace them!'

'But I need them for the work—'

'Yes, you've told me about your wonderful ark that's going to save us from a flood that'll never happen. You've made me a laughing stock! The other women snigger as I walk past. And the estate workers think you're stark staring crazy.'

'But everything's going so well.'

'For you it is! Meanwhile I'm trying to look after your estate and raise your family! A fine husband you've turned out to be – my mother was right when she warned me about you!'

'But I'm—'

'And our best workers are tied up in this lunacy. All I've got left are boys and toothless old men. The

44

harvest's been a shambles; we'll be lucky to get half the grain we had last year. It's rotting in the fields waiting for someone to reap it! If we go hungry it'll serve you right. There's only so much we women can do – and what about your sons, what are you going to leave them when you die? If we go on like this we'll finish up as slaves. We might as well move into a tent right now!'

He tried to put an arm round her, but she pushed him away.

'Leave me alone! I'm going back to the boys. Carry on playing your silly games if you must, but don't drag me into them!'

After she had left, he sat in his tent until nightfall. He felt utterly alone.

'I wanted her help and support. How can I keep going if she, of all people, won't stand by me?'

But then he realised how bizarre the site must have looked to her.

'Did I imagine it all? Perhaps I am mad. Why did the Holy One have to pick on me?'

After a restless night he woke knowing he must go straight home. Zillah was waiting for him and fell sobbing into his arms.

'I'm so ashamed! I knew all the time you were right about the flood and now I've had a dream about it. I let you down in front of all your men. Can you ever forgive me?'

8

'Reu, where can I get bronze tools from?'

It was dusk and Noah was looking frustrated.

'But, Master, what's wrong with Eber's stuff?'

'Those flint axes are fine for cutting scrub, but they're no good on bigger stuff. I need bronze for the next stage of the work.'

'The next stage, Master?'

'We've got to fell and shape a huge number of trees; we can't do that with flint. I've tried buying bronze from my neighbours, but there's none for sale. Every piece is a family heirloom.'

'Perhaps the Cainites will come down here on a trading mission.'

'That would help, but I need those tools now.'

'If we knew their secret, Master, we could make some ourselves!'

Noah looked at him hard. 'Be careful what you say. If they thought we were prying, I shudder to think what might happen.'

'So, Master, what can we do?'

'I don't know. Short of going there ourselves to buy, not much.'

'But you bought those cattle up there, didn't you?'

'Yes, people had been talking about trading with them for years, but I actually did it.'

'You were brave, Master.'

'Young and foolhardy, more like. I wouldn't like to try that again.'

But when Noah woke next day, he knew that was precisely what the Holy One was ordering him to do. First he would have to tell Zillah, and to his amazement she smiled.

'I don't want you to go, but if you must you must. Seth can look after us.'

His mouth dropped open. It was a miracle! Now he could start planning.

'I must take grain and oil for barter,' he thought, 'but I ought to take gold as well, although it'll mean selling some of my land. I suppose I might let those fields over the river go.'

The sale went through very quickly and he received three gold ingots. They fitted nicely in a money belt he wore day and night under his robe. But Zillah was indignant; her conciliatory mood had worn thin.

'Noah, I wanted to build houses for the boys over there but you let the land go without even asking me.'

'I'm sorry, dear. I didn't think you'd miss it.'

She sniffed. 'There's been a lot of talk. The servants think you're hard up and they are looking for other employers!'

But he had another problem: would he be able to recruit some volunteers to go with him? He gathered his men and offered them double pay, but as soon as he mentioned the Cainites there was a shocked silence and the men avoided his eye.

Then Tiras spoke. 'Count me in, Master! I'm not scared of the Cainites. I'm worth ten of them!'

Noah's relief was enormous. 'I'll be glad to have you!'

'Well, Master, it's high time someone stood up to them! And I hear they've got some fancy slave girls up there!'

Then Javan, an older man, joined in. 'I'll come too. You've been good to us, Master, and you've got the luck of the gods.'

'That's right!' someone else called. 'Remember how he dealt with all those folk in the Pitch Lands?'

That was the turning point, and soon Noah had his party.

They took one raft and set off upriver. For the first eight days they retraced the route to the Pitch Lands, but beyond the village things were unfamiliar and the men became uneasy since nobody seemed to be around. However, the river teemed with life, flocks of fowl erupting into the air, and once they saw a pile of droppings and some huge spoor leading up the bank. Javan looked at them carefully.

'Hippo, I reckon. You don't want to tangle with one of them!'

On another occasion, when they paused at midday Jerah, one of the younger men, went for a swim.

'Be careful!' Reu shouted.

'I'll be fine. I'll keep close to the raft.'

Then suddenly the water boiled, and a scaly monster broke the surface. Jerah screamed briefly as huge jaws seized his legs and dragged him under. Then, as the men watched horrified, the stream was stained red.

'In the name of Tiamat, what was that?' Tiras gasped.

'That must have been what they call a crocodile,' Javan groaned. 'I've heard talk of them, but that's the first I've ever seen – and may it be the last! I reckon we should sacrifice to Marduk to ask his protection.'

Two days later Tiras, who had been leading the party, hurried back to Noah.

'Look! Along there, Master – men coming our way!'

It was a party of ten, heavily armed, and as they approached they hailed Noah's party.

'You must pay a toll to pass here. What have you got?'

'Let's kill them!' Tiras whispered. 'If they get away with this, everyone will want their cut!'

'No! There must be more of them around, and anyway we've got to come back this way. I don't want to find an army blocking my route!'

Eventually it cost two sacks of corn, and Noah shook his head.

'I hope this doesn't happen often, or we won't have anything left to eat or barter with.'

The river became narrower, and one morning they crossed a stream pouring down from the hills. There, in the distance, Noah noticed a mountain with two peaks which he recognised from his dream.

'Remember this place,' he said to Reu. 'We'll be coming here again to cut wood!'

On the twelfth day they reached a cataract with an island just below it. Noah looked round carefully.

'This is where I came all those years ago to buy cattle from the Cainites. We'll have to walk from here to Tubal-Cain's city. But I can't remember which path to take.'

While they were unloading the raft, Noah took some men to reconnoitre. Suddenly they saw a youth and Tiras grabbed him. He shook with fear, but when Noah offered him some grain, he pointed to a track leading towards the mountains. Then he scuttled away into the bushes.

When the men were ready, Noah called Reu aside.

'I want you to stay here in charge of the raft and oxen.'

'Very good, Master, but I was hoping to come with you.'

'I'm sorry, but we must make sure everything's safe and you're the only man I can trust. I'll leave you four men, and I suggest you get the oxen and raft over to that island. You'll be safer there. If we're not back in a fortnight, go home without us.'

Next morning the men made an offering to the gods while Noah prayed to the Holy One. Then they shouldered their packs.

'Those look pretty heavy,' said Reu.

Noah nodded. 'Maybe, but we'll need all that stuff, I reckon.'

They toiled up one hill after another, only to plunge again into deep valleys, helping each other over the steepest parts. On the second night Noah spoke to Tiras.

'It's strange. We haven't seen anyone since we started, but I feel we're being watched.'

'Yes, Master. I saw fresh footprints on the track, and don't tell me the birds stole the sack of grain we lost yesterday!'

Next day they entered a gorge. The track ran along a precipice while a river cascaded far below. Eventually they reached a place where the route was blocked by a stockade. It had a gate at the bottom, but as they approached this slammed shut.

'Well,' said Noah, 'I remember this. It's the entrance to Tubal-Cain's city, but they don't seem too happy to receive visitors!'

Then a man appeared at the top of the stockade.

'What do you want?'

'We've come here to buy bronze.'

'Wait there!'

He disappeared, leaving them standing nervously. Noah walked back along the path to relieve himself and, making sure no one was watching him, transferred one of the gold ingots into his sleeve.

As he came back he heard dogs, then the door creaked open and a huge man appeared, armed with a club. He beckoned impatiently to Noah.

'Don't show any fear,' he told himself as the door slammed shut behind him, but his palms were wringing wet.

He was in a courtyard with 20 armed men. The dogs, the largest he had ever seen, snarled viciously and hurled themselves forward until they choked on their collars. The huge man spat at them, and as one sprang he smashed its head in. Instantly the other dogs leapt on it and tore it apart.

Noah watched horrified, but then the man beckoned through a door into a guardroom. There he found an old man wearing a black robe with a huge pendant round his neck.

'So, you've arrived at last!' he sneered. 'We expected you yesterday.'

Noah blinked.

'Don't look surprised! We could have set our army on you and you wouldn't have known a thing till we slit your throat!'

'But we come in peace. I want to buy bronze tools.'

'That's a new one! Not many snivelling sons of Seth visit us! But wait till I get instructions.'

'But what about my men?'

'We'll bring them in here. But they'll have to put their weapons down first. We're a very peaceable people. It wouldn't be nice if our guests attacked us!'

Noah heard the stockade door creaking open and the barking of the dogs rose in a crescendo. His men laid down their weapons and baggage and were ushered into the guardroom where they squatted on the floor supervised by two guards. One man was clutching his arm where a dog had bitten it.

It was a tight squeeze and soon the room became uncomfortably warm. Once Noah shifted to relieve cramp in his leg and a guard ordered him to sit still.

He forced himself to ignore the discomfort and watched a tiny patch of sunlight moving slowly across the wall.

Suddenly the dogs began howling and he started to panic. Without weapons he and his men were quite defenceless, and despite the heat he instinctively drew his cloak round him.

A guard laughed. 'They're starving out there and they like their meat fresh!'

Then to his horror the door opened very slowly.

9

It was Black Robe.

'Come with me. Your men will stay here. My servants will carry your goods.'

Suddenly there was a disgusting smell. Guards were driving some slaves into the courtyard. Although it was cold, they were naked, with ribs that stood out, limbs like sticks and skin covered in festering sores. They shuffled over to Noah's stuff.

'Pick it up! Careful or we'll have the hide off you!'

The loads were heavy and the slaves could hardly lift them. Noah cringed as he heard the guards' curses, the crack of whips and faint groans.

Black Robe saw and laughed. 'You may be next, old man!'

They set off and soon the valley widened out, then Noah heard a thud. A slave had collapsed. The guard whipped him, but the man merely writhed, so taking a knife the guard ripped open the man's belly, spilling his entrails on the ground. Then he ordered another slave to pick up the sack.

'Are you leaving him there?' Noah asked Black Robe.

'Don't worry. The dogs will clear it up.'

'But he's still alive!'

'Not when they've done!'

The other slaves must already have been anticipating teeth tearing through their flesh, and Noah wished he could give them some hope. But Black Robe had read his thoughts.

'Keep your eyes off our slaves!'

Ahead a track branched off, leading to a hole in the cliff, and close by was a grey building with a huge column of black smoke rising from it.

'That must be where they get the magic rock and turn it into bronze,' he thought.

'Don't dawdle.' Black Robe was looking at him suspiciously.

Then at last they arrived in front of a palace which was almost hidden by trees.

'This is Naamah's residence, the sister of Tubal-Cain,' Black Robe explained. 'You are privileged to be here. Come with me. We'll leave your stuff out here.'

He was hustled through an entrance hall into a side room filled with soldiers. Then an elderly man came in and the soldiers stood up and bowed. He was bent over and Noah's first impression was of a mass of white hair, but when he sat down, he looked up with piercing blue eyes.

'What's your name?'

'Noah, son of Lamech, of the clan of Enoch.'

'Where are you from?'

'The Great Valley. I have an estate there.'

'Why are you spying on us?'

'But I'm not. I've come here to buy bronze tools.'

'What do you want, spy?'

'I'm not a spy. As I said, I came to buy bronze tools and I can offer the finest grain and oil in exchange.'

The man jerked his head towards Black Robe. 'Bring his goods here.'

Black Robe returned with two men carrying some sacks and jars.

'Open them!'

A guard slashed a sack with his spear and the man took some grain, running it through his fingers onto the floor.

'And the oil!'

A servant pulled a bung from a jar and he sniffed it.

'The most I can offer is one bronze axe head for the lot.'

As Noah opened his mouth to protest, he added, 'That's my final offer!'

Noah groaned, realising how much grain and oil he had given for one axe head!

'Did you bring anything else?'

Reluctantly, he reached in his sleeve, pulling out the ingot.

'I have one piece of gold.'

The man examined it carefully and felt its weight before biting it.

'We might give you another axe head for this.'

'But that's robbery! It's worth far more!'

Then two guards grabbed him. The man smiled, but his eyes were like ice.

'Search him!'

In a moment they had pulled his robe up around his shoulders and ripped his money belt off. Then the guards started laughing.

'Quiet!'

Noah pulled down his robe, feeling humiliated and blushing like a girl.

They had placed all his gold on the floor. The old man was savouring the moment.

'Three pieces. You haven't been straight with us, but we'll be generous!'

Black Robe disappeared, returning with a small bundle, and the old man emptied it beside the gold. There were three bronze axe heads and an adze blade.

'There you are! Aren't we kind?'

Noah was speechless. He had been comprehensively cheated! The sale of his precious land and the dangerous journey had been for nothing. He would never be able to buy enough tools now.

'Take these before I change my mind,' the old man said. 'I could kill you right now and no man or god could stop me. I wouldn't come here again; I might not be so friendly next time!'

They gave him the bundle of tools, but it felt desperately light. Then he noticed the old man's arm.

He wore a grey bracelet, the most precious metal in the world – iron!

'An eye for quality, I see! But we don't sell this to riff-raff like you!'

Then the guards hustled Noah outside. All his goods had gone, but before he could protest they were marching him back down the valley. As they passed the place where the slave had died, he noticed a dark red patch swarming with flies.

When they reached the stockade his men were released from the guard house and picked up their weapons. Then the door crashed behind them and they were herded down the road.

Now Noah was overwhelmed by a sense of failure. How could he tell Zillah what had happened and how his sale of the land had been for nothing? But worse still, he was overcome with shame and anger at the way he had been treated and by the fear that he might still be pursued and forced into slavery.

They walked until sunset when they reached a place where the gorge opened out. They made a fire although they had no food, but no one felt like talking. Just as he was going to sleep, Noah heard men running down the path and saw flaming torches.

He waited until everything was quiet, but then he heard another noise like an animal scrabbling over the rocks behind him. As his men investigated, he lit a brand

and saw someone pinioned by two men, while Tiras held a flint knife to his throat.

It was a young man. His eyes gleamed in terror, his chest heaved and the smell of sweat was overpowering.

'Let him go, but see he doesn't escape.'

They dragged him to his feet, but then his knees buckled and he fell.

'Get some water! Use my drinking horn!'

They slopped some over his face before letting him drink. Then he looked around in panic. 'Don't let them get me! They'll kill me!'

'Don't worry, you're among friends. Are you in trouble with the Cainites?'

He nodded.

'We don't like them either. We won't let them get you. But who are you anyway?'

He stared at Noah. 'You don't know what you're doing! If they catch me here, they'll butcher the lot of you! Slowly!'

'But you're a Cainite?'

'Yes. Irad, son of Mehujael, born and bred here.'

'We've come from the Great Valley to trade.'

'Yes, I saw you today while I was hiding near the gate. I thought they'd kill you. If you knew anything about this place you wouldn't come within three days' journey!'

'Were they chasing you just now? We thought they were after us.'

Irad sighed. 'Yes, it's me. I've been hiding from them for days. I got out at dusk by climbing round the stockade – pretty steep, those cliffs! Thought I'd got away but a guard spotted me and I had to run for it. Then I tripped and gashed my leg and that slowed me down.'

'You're safe now.'

'No, it's all up for me. They'll be setting up checkpoints and as soon as it's light they'll come for me with dogs. They'll search everywhere and they'll never give up till they get me.'

'But why are they so worried about you?'

'I was in charge of the foundry. That's where we make the bronze and iron. I know all their secrets, so they can't afford to let me escape.'

'But what did you do?'

'I had a row over a woman – she was a chief's daughter and her father sent his heavies round to warn me off. So I stuck a knife in one.'

'You can come with us; they'll never notice an extra man.'

'Thanks – but I'm heading for the hills.'

'You won't get far with that leg. Stay with us till dawn. You'll break your neck if you try climbing in the dark.'

Tiras was agitated. 'Master, do what he says. We want to get home in one piece. Why throw our lives away for a Cainite?'

Noah shook his head. 'I've never turned away anyone in need yet and I won't start now! The Holy One's sent this man to us and he'll keep us all safe. Now let's get to sleep!'

10

The deer saved them.

Noah saw it at first light, grazing near the path.

'Can you kill it for me?' he whispered to Tiras. He reached for his bow and the deer took the arrow in the throat.

The men woke in panic.

'Quiet!' Noah whispered. 'Carry that deer down to the road and spill as much blood as possible. Irad give me your cloak.'

He daubed it in blood and ripped the seams.

'What are you doing?' he complained.

'I want the Cainites to think a lion killed you. If they think you're dead we may be able to smuggle you out of here.'

Then they dragged the deer back up the hill and hid it in a hollow. Noah had a last look around. 'We'll be all right if they don't discover that!'

Then they found Irad a spare cloak, but as they began walking down the road they met the men who had guarded them the day before.

'So it's you again. Stop there while we count you to make sure no one's missing.'

Noah broke into a sweat, but just then there was a shout and an officer appeared.

'We're too late. A lion's got him! I found his cloak. Back to your posts, quick!'

They waited until the guards disappeared before trudging on. Noah kept looking over his shoulder until Tiras spoke. 'You still worried, Master? They'd have got us by now if they were going to. That trick of yours with the deer was brilliant.'

'I'm worried we've got away too easily! And I wish we hadn't lost our food.'

'Pity we didn't bring some of that deer with us. I fancy a steak!' said Tiras, smiling at Noah's look of disgust.

When they reached the river, they saw the raft by the island but nobody was around.

'Typical!' Tiras jeered. 'We're starving and they're sleeping off their last meal!'

But then Reu appeared with two men and they poled the raft across.

'Sorry to keep you waiting, Master. We had a spot of trouble. Two days back we saw some men coming across in a reed boat so we lay low.'

'Were they after the oxen?'

'Oh yes!'

'Did you lose any?'

'No, the idiots managed to stampede them, and while this was going on we took our chance and killed three of them. Then the rest swam for it.'

'Have they been back?'

'No, Master! But I've a nasty feeling they'll have another go. That's why we hid till we knew it was you.'

They set off downriver immediately and camped at dusk. Tiras was stamping around, impatient for food.

Reu laughed. 'Hey! Leave the cook alone or you'll wait all the longer. We'll give you double rations tonight – we can't have you looking half-starved for your lady loves!'

Afterwards, Noah and Irad sat by the embers of the fire.

'Those tools I bought aren't up to much,' Noah confessed.

'Let me have a look at them.'

He threw fresh wood on the fire while Noah brought him the bundle. Then he examined each item in turn.

'They cheated you, right enough. This stuff's rubbish. It'll buckle as soon as you try using it.'

'Well, I might as well chuck it in the river!'

'It's not as bad as that. I could melt these down and make you a couple of good ones.'

For the first time in days Noah smiled. 'But what would you need?'

'Stones for a furnace, charcoal and some clay. Oh yes, some wood and cow hide for bellows. But it'd have to be somewhere secret that our Cainite friends don't know about.'

'You'd be safe on my estate.'

'No, people would talk and my folk would be prepared to slaughter whole villages if it kept their secrets safe.'

'But there's my old home in the mountains on the edge of the world. No one goes there.'

Irad came back with them to the settlement, much to Zillah's annoyance.

'What do you think you're doing, Noah, bringing that savage into this house? We won't be safe in our beds! And I don't like the way he smells!'

Irad also seemed uncomfortable, and one day he announced in front of all the men, 'I reckon I best be moving on. I'll try my luck downriver as far away from the Cainites as I can get.'

A couple of days later, Noah set off to see the old ones, taking Japheth and Ham with him and, to his servants' surprise, pack animals loaded with clay and charcoal.

'They're short of pottery and want to make more,' he told Zillah.

'But why not do it here? And what the boys will get up to when they're out of my sight!'

The heavily loaded animals slowed them down and it was the fourth afternoon before they reached the homestead.

Irad was watching from the edge of the forest, having trailed them the whole way. He had to wait until dark before crossing the open moorland, although it was bitterly cold.

When he finally reached the homestead, he heard his name being called softly. Noah showed him a room with a fire, meal and sleeping mat, but all too soon he was woken again, then he and Noah set out in the dark shouldering large bundles of food. They climbed towards the distant mountains, black against the first grey of dawn, and at sunrise paused to drink from a brook.

'Is it much further?' Irad asked nervously.

'No. We'll be turning off the path in a moment. Just there beyond that large rock.'

They turned onto a sheep track running downhill into a hidden valley.

'See those trees?' Noah said. 'They grow here because it's sheltered. But the top branches bend where the wind catches them.'

Then Noah pointed to a ruined hut. 'Our shepherds lived there, but maybe you could repair it.'

Irad nodded. 'It shouldn't take long to make it weatherproof and fit a new door.'

'I'll bring my sons over soon with the clay and charcoal. I hope the men won't ask any awkward questions.'

'Thank you. I'll need more food.'

'I'll arrange that. Here's our old bronze axe. You can use it to cut the wood for the roof. I'll be back soon.'

'Don't be too long.' Irad tried to sound casual, but he spoke rather quickly. It was easy to believe in ice demons here.

When Noah, Japheth and Ham returned two days later, they found the hut had been re-roofed with turf, but there was no sign of Irad. And to his disgust Noah found a clay figure with blood and feathers scattered around it.

'He's made an idol and is sacrificing to it.'

Ham shrugged. 'Don't be too hard on him, Dad. It could be quite lonely up here.'

At that moment, Irad burst out of the trees at the top of the valley laughing and shouting.

'He's gone mad!' Japheth exclaimed.

In a moment he was dragging Noah up the path and pushing through bushes. He stopped in front of a rock face. It looked like any other outcrop, brown and bluish green.

'This is the magic rock like we've got at home. I can make you bronze right here!'

Noah rubbed his forehead. 'I've been worried sick about how to get proper tools, and the answer's been under my nose. And the Holy One's given me the one man who knows what to do!'

'Shall I start now?'

'Fine, but don't you need help?'

'I'd better do it myself. If your men find out I'm making bronze, it's bound to get back to the Cainites. But I could teach you what to do.'

'Thank you, but I've got too much to do.'

'Well, let your boys become my apprentices.'

'Hmm... I wonder what their mother will think. And how about the servants?'

'Find us a few sheep and you can always say they're learning to be shepherds!'

11

In years to come, the boys would remember this as the happiest, most carefree time of their lives, despite all the hard work. They learned to mine ore, burn charcoal and smelt bronze as well as looking after the sheep.

Once Irad killed and roasted a deer. Ham nearly gagged when he saw the meat; he had never encountered any before. And yet the smell was rather pleasant, and when nobody was looking he cut himself a small piece. It tasted quite as good as it smelled.

In the evenings they enjoyed their own entertainments. Irad showed them how to make a pipe from reeds and taught them how to play it. Then he carved a lyre, stringing it with gut from the deer, and sang them a sad love song.

'This is the music we had at home. They say that Jubal himself composed that tune.'

One late summer evening as he was playing, Japheth saw a shooting star falling towards the moor above the valley.

'If we could find where that came down we might get some iron. Perhaps we might even make a bracelet like the one father saw that chief wearing.'

Irad grunted. 'Well, that's what we tell outsiders. Iron is a gift from heaven, thrown down in the occasional stone.'

Ham was intrigued. 'What do you mean, you tell outsiders? Can you find it anywhere else?'

Reaching inside his cloak Irad pulled out a skin purse containing a small black stone. 'We get our iron from here, but the only place you can find this is back home.'

Japheth took the stone and looked at it carefully. 'But I've seen rock just like this. It's over the mountains in the empty valley.'

'Guarded by ice demons?'

'I've never met any. But I've seen this rock right enough – a huge cliff of it!'

After a lot of persuasion Irad agreed to have a look for himself. It was a steep climb, but eventually the empty valley was spread out below them, endless moorland with an autumnal wind ruffling the rough grass. He did not want to go any further until he spotted the black cliff and then he rushed forward. Soon he had collected as much ore as they all could carry.

Iron smelting was a much harder job than making bronze, but eventually Irad produced a piece of dark grey metal. 'It's not as pretty as that chief's bracelet, but it's the same stuff. It's better than bronze for making knives and axe heads but the Cainites have a monopoly on it. If they ever saw you had even the smallest bit, you'd be dead! I could make a couple of bracelets out of this, but you'd have to keep them up here.'

The winter drove them out. The wind howled through countless crevices in the hut and the snow fell so thickly they could hardly walk.

Irad was concerned. 'We must get out of here soon, or the next snowfall will trap us completely and we'll starve if we can't get more food!'

It took all day to fight their way back to the homestead, loaded down with the bronze they had made and herding the sheep through snowdrifts. On their arrival the old ones gave Ham and Japheth a warm welcome, but Irad had to hide in an outhouse.

As they left next morning, Lamech took the boys to one side. 'Take care what you say when you get home. There have been strange rumours about you, suggesting you are possessed by ice demons. It would be most unfortunate if the truth became known.'

Once again Irad followed them, but he had decided to spend the winter in the city. So on his return Ham begged his parents to let him go there too.

Zillah was disappointed. 'If you must go, behave yourself. I'm only agreeing so long as you stay with my cousin Seba. I don't want you wandering around on your own.'

Irad was very cheerful when he met up again with Ham. 'I've had enough of being cooped up on the edge of nowhere! The solitary life doesn't suit me.'

'Yes, it's going to be good. It's the first time I've been to the city without Dad keeping an eye on me!'

Irad put a hand on his shoulder. 'But it's not all fun and games, you know. There are dangerous folk around. Be on your guard, and remember, I've got enemies. If I get into a fight keep out of the way!'

'But I—'

'I mean it! There are folk who'll stop at nothing if they know I'm alive. If anyone attacks me, run for your life. I don't want my knowledge dying with me. You owe it to me to stay alive and show others how to make bronze and iron.'

As they entered the city, Irad found some temple prostitutes.

'Are you joining us, Ham?'

'Well... eh... oh, there's a friend of mine across the street. I think I'll have a word with him.'

As they chatted, Ham glanced back occasionally. Irad had taken a lyre and was playing for the women. It was a Cainite song about a young man in love.

Suddenly a commotion broke out behind him. Cainite soldiers were pushing through the crowd! He must warn Irad. There was not a moment to lose!

But it was too late. As they tried to seize him he slipped out of his cloak, leaving it in their hands, and gained precious moments by overturning a bench in their path. He ran down one street with the soldiers in hot pursuit, dodging in and out of the market stalls. But more Cainites were coming the other way and he was cornered. They killed him there, hacking him into pieces.

Ham watched in horror, then turned away and vomited in a doorway.

12

'But what's all this work for, Master?'

Reu had asked the question Noah dreaded, but he owed him an explanation.

'Well, it started with a vision from the Holy One.'

'You mean your nightmares?'

'Yes. This work is only a beginning; I want to build a kind of boat, what I call an ark, on top.'

'A boat, Master? I heard something but I thought it was a joke.'

'No, it's true. A huge boat lying in this space we staked out.'

'But you'd never launch it!' Reu laughed then looked embarrassed. 'Beg pardon, Master, but it won't fit on the river. You'd need a flood to move it, like the one the men talk about.'

'A flood?'

'It's an old story. Men were so noisy they kept the gods awake at night, so they decided to drown them in a flood.'

'There is going to be a flood, but it's the Holy One who will send it. And not because we're noisy, but as a punishment for the dreadful things we do.'

'What dreadful things?'

'Like the worship in the temple? What sort of god enjoys seeing a baby dragged from its mother's breast and thrown in a fire?'

'We've always done that!'

'The poor mother has to watch it burn and try to feel honoured! I saw it once and I'll never forget the look in that girl's eyes!' Noah's anger burned. 'Then, there's the way you get blind drunk and use those temple prostitutes. It may be fun for the men but how about those girls and boys?'

'Are you getting at me because I sold two of my daughters to the temple?' said Reu, red-faced.

'Well, weren't you worried what would happen to them?'

'They have enough to eat. We've got a lot of mouths to feed and have to make ends meet. Begging your pardon, Master; I'm not saying you don't pay well!'

'And then there's the violence. I can't go anywhere without a bodyguard.'

'That's being sensible, Master.'

'Aren't you upset that people are killed for no reason at all and their bodies get dumped in the street?'

'I say, "Mind your own business".'

Then Noah remembered the woman he had killed and winced.

'You worry too much, Master.'

'The Holy One worries too. That's why he's sending a flood to wipe out these wicked people.'

'So that's why you want the boat? To escape?'

'Yes.'

'But what about everyone else, Master?'

'I'm afraid they'll drown.'

Suddenly Reu's eyes blazed.

'So that's it! We build you a boat to save your skin, and you leave us to die! A funny sort of god you've got! He worries about a few babies being sacrificed, but he's willing to kill the rest of us. I'll slave my guts out for you, then you'll turn around and watch me swim!'

He turned away, but Noah caught his arm.

'Listen! This boat's going to be huge. There's room for you and for anyone else to join us. I won't turn anyone away!'

Reu took a while to calm down.

'Even if there is a flood, Master – and I'm not saying there will be – you won't want my family under your feet.'

'We'd be delighted to have you, although you've plenty of time to build your own boat. But I really hope the ark won't be needed; if people realise the Holy One's serious about judging them, they may repent and he won't send a flood after all.'

'So what good would your boat be then?'

'None at all. I'd have spent my money and look a fool. But I'd rather that than watch everyone die!'

Afterwards Noah sat thinking. 'Why can't he understand? He's intelligent... Maybe I was like that before the Holy One spoke to me. Anyway, it's high time I told the men what I'm doing and offer them refuge.'

At last the cradle was complete, with ramps at one end so that timber could be dragged on top. A village had sprung up for the labourers beyond the estate boundary; the prospect of work had attracted many men from the city.

Now Noah called a planning meeting. 'We're going to start collecting materials to build the ark. Pallu, you must make a lot more journeys to get pitch. Then we'll need rope.'

Reu smiled. 'That's easy, Master. The river's thick with reeds.'

'Good, but we need to stockpile it now so there won't be any delays when we start building.'

Reu sent gangs of men to cut the reeds with wooden scythes embedded with flint. These were plaited into long strands, then several of them were twisted together to form rope. But the biggest challenge was finding suitable timber in huge quantities.

'This is the place!' Noah called.

They were upriver, where the stream he had noted earlier joined the main river.

Reu frowned. 'Are you sure?'

'Yes, that mountain over there with the twin peaks is the sign. I pointed it out to you when we were going to the Cainites.'

'I remember. You must know this area.'

'Not really, but the Holy One showed it to me in a dream.'

Reu stared. 'You mean you brought us all this way to cut timber because of a dream? Where are your trees, Master?'

'You'll see. Once we've headed up this stream.'

It was hard going; the current was strong and there were many rocks. Worse still, the oxen had to struggle through the shallows since there was no path. But suddenly they found themselves in a forest, with magnificent stands of cypress on either bank towering high above them.

They tied up below some rapids and prepared to camp on a sand spit since it was the only open space.

Reu looked doubtful. 'What happens if the stream rises, Master?'

'We'll shift everything back onto the rafts, but once we've cleared some trees we'll make a proper camp on the bank. However, before we do anything, I'd like to know if anyone lives around here.'

The night passed peacefully, but next morning Reu spotted a shaman coming through the trees.

He was an old man in a skin robe and necklace of skulls. Lifting his staff, he croaked, 'Do you come in peace?'

'We do.'

'Put your weapons down.'

Noah hesitated. Would they be at the mercy of men hidden in the trees?

'Put your weapons down!'

Noah turned to his men. 'Do as he says. Pile them up over there.'

They obeyed, glancing nervously at the stranger. Then Noah and Reu walked forward to meet him. His hair was matted with mud, his cloak was filthy and he stank like a stag in rut.

'There!' whispered Reu, pointing to the trees. 'There must be at least thirty men in there!'

'Try not to show fear,' Noah said to himself, as he turned around slowly, presenting his back as an easy target. Then he beckoned to Reu's son.

'Cush, get me a bowl of corn for our friend here, and make it quick!'

The youth hesitated, his lip quivering.

'Come on, lad. What's keeping you?'

Cush nearly dropped the bowl as he walked forward, holding the gift right out in front of him. Noah noticed his revulsion. The stench was overpowering.

The shaman took a pinch of grain and chewed it with blackened teeth. Then he beckoned to Noah.

'Come. We have matters to discuss.'

Noah turned to his men. 'Reu, you come with me. Pallu, you're in charge here.'

As they reached the trees, the armed men closed ranks behind them.

13

The path was steep, and Noah was out of breath by the time they reached a clearing. There was a large round hut with a low doorway and the shaman crawled inside. Noah and Reu followed reluctantly.

It was lit by two lamps and smelled terrible. But what Noah really noticed was the deep sense of evil.

'Let me introduce myself. I am Ki, high priest of the Calneh.'

'I am Noah, son of Lamech.'

'Noah. That's a powerful name.'

Then he remembered that sorcerers never disclose their real names in case it gave others power over them. Had he been wise to give his own?

Ki clapped his hands and an old woman entered and handed him a large beaker. He drank deeply then passed it to Noah.

'It is our custom that our guests share our cup.'

He took a small sip; it tasted of sour milk.

'So, Noah, son of Lamech, why are we honoured with your presence?'

He decided to come straight to the point.

'I need timber, and you have large forests. I would like to fell some trees.'

'What a pity! I could have saved you the journey. Our trees are the finest in the world but I cannot let you have any.'

'I'll pay a fair price.'

'Indeed, but each one is sacred since it holds the spirit of an ancestor. If it is cut down that soul is thrown into the abyss.'

'But what do your ancestors do when their tree dies?'

Ki cackled, making Noah's scalp tingle. 'A good question! Now if I perchance let you cut down a tree you would have to appease its spirit.'

Noah groaned. He must compromise his beliefs again. 'Would you tell my foreman what is required?'

'Indeed.'

And what would you charge?'

'As guardian of the holy mysteries, I may not ask for reward. But perhaps the gods might fancy some sacks of grain and a few cattle.'

Then he noticed a dagger in Noah's waistband. 'May I see it?'

He examined it carefully. 'Ah! Bronze! Sacred to the gods! Do you have any bronze axes?'

'Yes, a few.'

'Trees cut down with these release their spirits into joy! You could have more timber if you used them. And perhaps you might offer some to the gods?'

'But what happens if they fall into the hands of the Cainites?'

'The Cainites are a strange people. They say they do not fear anyone, but since I put a curse on them they won't come anywhere near us!'

The haggling went on, but at last they struck hands on a deal; Noah would give Ki two bronze axes as well as grain and oxen. When he crawled out of the hut he was startled to see the sun was setting, but it was wonderful to breathe clean air again.

Noah was standing by the rafts when the first tree fell. He heard a shout and looked up to see it falling directly on top of him, but he managed to throw himself clear just in time.

Reu arrived at a run. 'I thought we'd killed you, Master!'

'It was my fault. I didn't realise how big that tree was.'

Soon the branches had been trimmed away and they began the laborious task of digging out the stump to clear the ground.

There was no singing around the fire that evening – the men were too exhausted – but the work soon fell into a rhythm. The finished timber was left floating in the stream secured by ropes to the bank, but one morning Noah discovered that three trees were missing.

Reu was apologetic. 'I'm sorry, Master, we didn't finish till after dark last night, and someone must have forgotten to tie them up properly.'

Noah groaned. 'They'll be in the river by now. We can't afford to lose any more; you'd better haul the rest onto the bank and stack them there.'

By summer they had made a large clearing. Then one day it rained heavily and Noah became uneasy.

'Reu, the stream's bound to rise. Shift the camp up the hill and take all the timber we've cut and lash it down. You'll also need to move the rafts.'

'But, Master, they're far too heavy to move.'

'Break them up and shift them in sections. They'll be swept away if they stay where they are.'

It was a brutal job in the pouring rain. The oxen churned the ground into a quagmire, and men and beasts floundered into old stump holes.

The rain continued relentlessly and by next morning the sandbar and most of the clearing were under water. There was no let up in the weather all day, and that evening the light faded early. Then Noah heard someone calling him.

It sounded more like a howl than a voice, and it cut through the steady drumming of rain on the roof. He saw a figure emerging from the wood and flinched, wondering if it was a ghost. Then he recognised Ki.

'You're committing sacrilege, cutting down the holy trees!' He shouted. 'The gods are furious. They'll drown us all!'

'No!' Noah replied. 'I've kept my side of the bargain and you must keep yours!'

'Blasphemer! Violator of the mysteries!' Then Ki began a falsetto chant.

The sound throbbed in Noah's head until he thought it would burst and he stood paralysed.

'I've cursed you, old man! You'll die tonight!'

Noah splashed back to his tent, conscious that his men were watching him. Of course, the curse was childish, but he was feeling a little unwell and his evening meal of uncooked grain looked rather unappetising.

Soon he became burning hot, lying naked on his bed and calling out in delirium. He drifted in and out of consciousness. Once when his mind cleared he saw the terrified face of Reu holding out a drinking horn.

'Take this, Master. You'll feel better in the morning.'

He forced some down but vomited it straight back. The lamp blew out and the darkness overwhelmed him. He dreamed he was back by the cradle, up to his waist in water as the rain thundered down. Ki was there too, laughing and jeering, looking like the evil one he had glimpsed in Eden.

'You'll never see your wife and sons again! Your god's given you up! Don't struggle any more!'

He felt as if he were being sucked into an abyss and his strength ebbed away. Then something or someone compelled him to speak.

'I know you, you liar! The Holy One sent me here and he'll save me! I curse you – in his name!'

Ki screamed. His body swelled until he was a giant stretching high above Noah. Then suddenly he burst into flames and was reduced to a small pile of ashes.

The tent glowed with light. A deep peace came over Noah and he slept.

Sunlight was streaming into his hut as he woke. Reu sat beside him, fast asleep, but he stirred as Noah got up.

'Are you all right, Master?'

'I feel fine.'

'I was so worried about you last night. But that draught of mine always does the trick; it was my grandmother's recipe!'

The woods steamed in the heat. The river had fallen and none of the timber had been lost. But Reu looked worried.

'Shall we stop? Ki doesn't want us to fell any more trees.'

'Forget him! Get the men back to work. We've lost enough time already!'

Ki appeared around midday, looking cautiously around the camp.

'I'm here!' Noah shouted. 'I'm not dead yet!'

A look of astonishment came over his face and he turned and ran.

Reu burst out laughing. 'He can't have moved that fast in years!'

The next two weeks were the most productive of all. The men worked enthusiastically, knowing they would be soon be going home. But then tragedy struck.

As one tree fell, its branches snagged in the boughs of a neighbour. A young man, Meshech, jumped forward.

'I'll get it! I see where it's caught.'

At that moment the branches supporting the tree gave way, and as Meshech tried to jump clear his feet slipped. His scream seemed to linger on as he was crushed.

His head was reduced to a shapeless mass of blood, bone fragments and brain, and by the time they hauled the tree trunk off him, his body was torn to pieces and his abdomen had burst. They buried him as best they could by the river with a piece of the tree that killed him.

For Noah it was a double blow: the loss of a young man, and the knowledge that the men would see this as a bad omen.

He summoned Reu. 'I think it's time we went home.'

'Yes, Master. The men think we've been cursed and wonder who's going to be next.'

It was time to settle up with Ki. He looked embarrassed when Noah arrived, but was happy to receive the promised grain, oxen and bronze axe heads.

'Will we have the pleasure of seeing you again?'

'Yes, we'll return next year if you are agreeable.'

14

'Noah, what are you doing? Playing with a toy boat like a two-year-old! There's mud all over your robe!'

Zillah stormed off, shaking her head.

Noah had wondered how to build the ark. He knew the size and that it had three floors, but he could not remember the details. Then he saw some boys playing with toy boats.

'That's it!' he shouted. 'I'll make a model!'

He constructed a raft from twigs tied together with straw, but when he tested it in the river it fell apart. So he tried again.

'What are you up to, Dad?'

It was Ham. Shamefacedly, Noah showed him his work.

'Dad – it's your ark! You're trying to see how to make it.'

He grabbed the model.

'It won't work like this. You need sinew to tie it together. And another layer of sticks on top laid the other way.'

The next raft hardly flexed when Ham dropped it into the water, and the knots held firm. But he was not satisfied.

'I think we need another layer of sticks on top. But weren't you building a boat?'

'Yes, well, more like a box really. We've got to fix walls around it but I don't know how to attach them to the base.'

'You can tie them, but you'll also need to brace them with struts slanting up from the base. I'll plug the cracks with wax; it's less messy than pitch at this stage.'

The new version was watertight, but Ham was still not satisfied.

'The walls aren't strong enough. They flex if you touch them. And we've forgotten those two extra decks which divide it into three floors.'

Then he exclaimed, 'That's it! Those floors and the roof will make the structure rigid. I'll have to throw this model away and start again.'

The new version was strong enough to stand on and it floated beautifully. But even that was not enough.

'It's too small to show details. We need something larger and someone who knows about timber.'

'What about Enosh? He's a natural with wood.'

With his help, Ham made a model of a section of the ark with the base, walls, decks and roof, together with the cross bracing and an external door.

'Is it all right, Dad?'

'Yes, Ham, this is just what I saw in my vision. All we need now are some plans on clay tablets, and some examples of the carpentry joints for the men to copy.'

Noah divided his workforce into three: Pallu would lead one group to collect pitch, Reu would be in charge of another getting timber, but who would supervise construction?

'There's Seth,' he thought, 'but Zillah wouldn't let him go and Ham's a bit young. I might try Tiras.'

Reu was not impressed. 'Master, you're running a risk with him.'

'Perhaps; but I'll start him on something small and see how he does. He can organise the oxen dragging timber up to the cradle.'

Tiras was in his element. The site was shrouded in dust and the noise was terrific as the drivers shouted and cracked their whips and the oxen bellowed in protest. But everyone responded well and worked faster than usual.

Once, Noah watched a huge trunk being dragged out of the water. The driver was flogging his oxen, unaware they were hindered by a broken branch snagging on the ground. He stepped forward to warn him.

'Don't get too close, Master,' Tiras called.

'I just want to tell that driver about the—'

Then the rope broke and snapped back, grazing Noah's cheek. Tiras leapt forward, grabbing the driver and forcing him to kneel. 'Forgive me, Master!' the driver begged.

Noah rubbed his cheek. There was blood on it. 'If that had been any closer I'd be dead!'

Then he picked up the rope. 'It's frayed! Didn't you check it this morning?'

'Tiras said not to bother. He said there wasn't time.'

Soon they had dragged the loose timber out and only the new rafts remained.

'Break those up,' Noah ordered, 'but don't cut the ropes. We'll need them again. And Tiras, I'm warning you, I don't want you slipping them a sharp flint when I'm elsewhere. I've seen you taking the easy way out before!'

Next morning Noah briefed him again.

'You can start work properly. I want a row of logs across the cradle; the alternate ones must stick out so we can tie them to the next row, and be sure to square off the ends so they butt together.'

'Leave it to me!'

Noah returned to find the men trying to fit two logs together. 'That won't do! You've got to get them a lot closer. And you've forgotten to cut grooves. When the ark floats, any exposed rope will be ripped off. And don't forget to seal the ties with pitch and cover them to keep the weather off.'

Noah inspected the work meticulously, often pointing to a suspect tie. 'Clean that one up and do it again.'

Next spring he left Tiras in charge of the site, while he accompanied Reu to cut more timber. Things went well.

They felled many trees and Ki did not refer to the unpleasantness of the previous year. But Noah was worried about Reu.

'I think he resents me taking him away from the ark; I can hardly get a word out of him. I won't be sorry to see Tiras again – he may not be so reliable but he's cheerful!'

When he eventually returned to the site, Noah was pleased to see that all the loose timber had been moved, but although it was mid-afternoon, only one man was around.

'Where's Tiras?'

The man sniggered. 'Off with his new woman! You won't see him today!'

Noah went on top of the cradle, getting down on his knees to examine the ties, then clambered down to examine them from beneath.

Early next morning he waited for the men. They sauntered in late with Tiras last of all. Then he called them together, watching as they shifted uneasily.

'I thought I could trust you!' he shouted. 'I spent months showing you what to do and I expected you to do a good job, but you've made a shambles of everything!'

Tiras started walking away, but he called him back.

'You've pushed the logs in anyhow, you haven't squared off the ends and you've left huge gaps. You've even used the scrap timber I'd kept for scaffolding!'

He waved a piece of rope. 'This is one of your ties; it came off in my hand and there's not a trace of pitch on it. You couldn't build a raft to carry cow dung! Either you rip everything out and do it again properly or none of you will ever work for me again!'

Noah took charge. It was a grim job, finding out how much needed to be repeated, and the men looked sullen.

That evening Tiras had disappeared, and they found he had taken a dozen young men and women with him.

Reu sighed. 'Don't say I didn't warn you, Master. All he's good for is swilling wine and chasing women.'

Several weeks later, Reu reported back to Noah. 'I've heard Tiras has got what was coming to him. He and his precious friends went to the city, like they owned it. He got a new woman, a concubine belonging to one of the Nephilim, no less! A posse came looking for him and they say he killed eight of them before they got him. A lot of men will sleep easier tonight!'

15

Noah chose Ehud as his new foreman.

'It's a tough job,' he warned. 'We've lost a lot of men, and it'll take time to clear up the mess. Watch the older men, they'll make a fool of you if they can.'

'I'll do my best, Master. And may I have Kenan to help me?'

'He's young too, and rather shy, but I'll give him a chance.'

Ehud and Kenan worked hard, checking every log laid by Tiras. Some were discarded and the others were reshaped, fitted back in position and sealed with pitch. Noah was delighted with their work and the way the men responded to them.

A rhythm developed: seasons for making rope, felling timber and collecting pitch. Row after row of logs was added, until the first layer was complete. But on the morning after a full moon they found a dead goat.

The din brought Noah hurrying from his tent. The men were in a panic. Even Ehud was scared.

'Master, it's... it's... by the cradle!'

A goat's head was impaled on a stake, with blood daubed over the bricks, and the belly was slit open with the entrails arranged in a fan shape.

The men were running away in terror, so Noah hitched up his robe and followed.

'What's got into you?' he gasped as he caught up with Javan, an older man.

'We're cursed! You saw the sign?'

'I don't believe that rubbish!'

'Master, Marduk's claimed the site. It's filled with demons. If we stay there we'll die!'

'Well, I'm sending those demons back where they belong! And I'm clearing up that mess before it starts stinking.'

'But if anyone touches it they'll be disembowelled on the spot!'

Noah felt sweat prickling his brow, then he remembered the night Ki had cursed him.

'Come on – I'll show you what that curse is worth!'

To his surprise, most of the men followed.

The goat was thick with flies, but he grabbed the stake and threw the head in the river. Then he bundled up the body, retching continually. The men watched in fascination, expecting something to rip him open as he dragged it into the water and ducking down rubbed himself clean. Then he took some water and washed the blood off the bricks.

The men were staring at him, so he lifted his arms and shouted.

'Holy One, protect my family, myself and everyone. I defy you, Marduk, to strike me dead in front of these men.'

Then he laughed. 'You've got no power! This place belongs to the Holy One!'

He spent the rest of the day praying and wondering if the men would stay. But next day, looking embarrassed, they still reported for work.

On the night of the next full moon, Noah woke suddenly, smelling wood smoke and hearing chanting.

Although he was frightened, he got up and stumbled out of his tent. He could see six dancing figures by the cradle in front of a fire.

The lookout had vanished so he roused the men himself. Then they crept forward, clutching their spears.

As he approached, he saw the dancers were women, stark naked, gleaming with oil and carrying torches. When they saw the men they shrieked, rushing forward like wildcats.

'Take them alive!' Noah shouted, and the men drove them into a corner with their spear butts. Their bodies were heaving from their exertion, and were covered in snake tattoos. Their shaved heads were doused in blood which had run down their faces and between their breasts and they had a deep musky smell.

The men were laughing and cheering. Then Kenan grabbed one girl by her breasts.

'Stop!' Noah shouted. 'I'll kill the next man who touches them. Ehud get some rope, tie them up and put them in that empty hut, then take three men and stand guard. The rest of you get that fire out!'

Blazing brushwood had been thrown on the cradle and some timbers had caught fire. Desperately the men pulled the burning beams from the brick piers and dumped them by the river.

Next day, Noah inspected the damage with Ehud.

'It could be worse. We'll have to rebuild one end of the cradle, but the ark's undamaged.'

It was time to check the prisoners. They were clothed and tied to wooden posts. One gave Noah a hard stare and wriggled her shoulders until her robe fell around her waist.

'Take a good look, old man! Better have me if you still can!'

'Cover her up!' he ordered, and a guard rearranged her robe while shielding himself from her spittle.

She was still staring, but her eyes were empty as if she was a ghost. She looked very young, but the evil one had sucked the life from her, robbing her of her childhood.

'Why did you do it?'

'He sent us. He hates you and won't let you build your boat. You were lucky last night but next time there'll be hundreds of us to finish the job!'

'You'll never do it! The Holy One's protecting us!'

She spat. 'You remember the goat? It was Marduk's curse and one day it'll reach you! You can't hide in your boat when the flood comes – because there won't be any boat!'

Noah turned away, but now instead of guilty desire he only felt grief for her.

'Go and get some sleep,' he told Shem. 'You've done an excellent job.'

He chose two older men to guard them, but when he returned that afternoon the door was open and the girls' clothes and ropes were scattered on the floor. He found the body of one guard badly mutilated, but the other was never seen again.

Despite his brave words, Noah was frightened, waiting for the women's return. Each full moon he kept watch, but on the fourth month he was so tired he fell asleep. Then Ehud called him around midnight.

'Master! They're coming! Thousands of them! Let's get out of here! Quick!'

'No, Ehud! We stay. Get the men up.'

Already he could see torches through the trees and a confused sound of screaming and shouting. His men crouched in the moonlight rigid with fear, but somehow he knew that he must see what was happening and he climbed to the lookout post on the tree, trying to forget the drop below.

The sight was appalling, a huge crowd of soldiers, and naked women gyrating to the sound of horns and drums coming towards him. This was the end of everything.

Suddenly, incredibly, they fell silent. They seemed to be staring at something, then they began screaming and running away as if chased by demons.

Very nervously Noah turned his head, but he could see nothing except the night sky and the full moon.

Eventually everything became quiet. Perhaps this was some trick, but eventually he carefully climbed down. There was no one around, but the road was littered with spears, cloaks, bags and spent torches.

'Ehud, get some men!' he shouted.

He began leading them along the road and soon they found a young girl gibbering with fear. Like the other women, she was naked, tattooed and daubed with blood, but she had a broken spear sticking into her thigh.

They made her a litter from branches and carried her back to the huts. Then she began screaming and throwing herself around so violently she nearly fell out.

'If only Reu was here, he'd know what to do,' Noah said. 'We'd better leave that spear in for now. Cover her up and give her some poppy juice to calm her.'

In the morning she was deathly pale and looked terrified, and it took a lot of coaxing to get her story.

'We came to burn your precious ark and to sacrifice all of you. We were almost here when we saw two horrible great men. Shining they were and higher than the trees and they had huge flaming swords in their hands. You won't let them get me?'

'You're safe with us.'

'Then everyone ran like the blazes, then this clumsy oaf of a soldier tripped me up and stuck me with his spear. Just left me there, he did!'

She died that evening, her body writhing as she tried to escape the thing sent to take her.

Then Noah remembered the cherubim who guarded the gate of Eden; now they must be protecting his ark.

A forest of pillars was rising at one end of the ark to support the next deck. Ham seemed to be everywhere, rushing around with his model and clay tablets and giving urgent instructions to Ehud and Kenan.

'Make sure you remember all the struts and cross-braces; it'll be difficult to fit them in later. Enosh! Make sure those pillars are four metres long and see that you square them off properly and you've cut all the sockets.'

Then he turned to the women. 'Before they bring the next load of timber, pack all the gaps between the logs with reeds. Push in as much as you can, then pound them with mallets before we get the pitch.'

At the mention of pitch they looked resigned. Their hair and clothes would reek for days.

One day Noah found Ham asleep with a chunk of bread still in his hand. He woke with a start. 'Sorry, Dad!'

Noah shook his head. 'Don't think I'm not grateful, Ham, for all you're doing, but don't wear yourself out!'

'I won't. I just want to get this job right. You know yesterday I caught the men putting on another layer of logs before any reeds had been packed in.'

'Isn't Ehud checking that?'

'He's supposed to, but he puts things off. He reckons he can fix mistakes later. I like to get it right first time.'

'Don't forget I put him in charge. He's getting annoyed that you keep interfering and he's even talked of quitting.'

'I'm sorry. I'll try not to bother him again.'

'By the way, I've noticed our tools are getting worn. How about you and Japheth making some more?'

'Are you trying to get rid of me, Dad?'

'I thought you could do with a break. And we do need more tools.'

Some weeks later, Ehud proudly took Noah to one end of the ark.

'Look, Master, this is what it'll all look like when it's finished: three layers of logs, everything tied in and sealed. All we need now is sand to cover the pitch.'

'Excellent! This feels really solid. But what are you doing about drainage?'

Ehud sounded puzzled. 'Ham didn't say anything about that.'

'There'll be a lot of water down here from leaks and spray. Leave some gaps in the top row of logs so the water will collect there rather than slopping about. And leave enough space so you can get a bucket in there to bail it out.'

Noah visited the old ones in the summer and went to the secret valley. He was alarmed to find Japheth had lost most of his hair.

'It's nothing, Father. I'm fine. It's all sorted out.'

'But what happened?'

'We sort of set fire to the cottage roof, but we got everything out before it fell in. You see we were running short of charcoal and tried using wood instead and a whole lot of sparks came out of the top.'

'Don't try that again!'

'No chance! We've built a new furnace well away from the cottage. But have a look at these axe heads! I know they're not up to Irad's standard... You know, it's funny but I keep expecting him to walk in the door... but how are things at the ark?'

'Not too bad, but soon we're going to need planks and I'm wondering how to cut them.'

'Why don't we make bronze saws? They'd be much better than the flint ones Eber makes.'

'Hmm... But I wouldn't like the Cainites to know how much bronze we have. Better just make a couple for now.'

As Noah sat with the old ones that evening, Lamech spoke.

'You look worried, my son.'

'Well, I'm wondering if I'll be able to finish building the ark.'

'But surely the Holy One called you to this work?'

'He did, but I don't think I have enough resources. I still need a huge amount of wood and Ki, that's the shaman, keeps raising the price.'

'The Holy One will provide.'

When Noah woke next morning, he was resigned to making a difficult decision.

'I must sell more land,' he told Lamech, 'although I hate doing it and I dread to think what Zillah will say. A whole tract upstream of the settlement must go.'

'Will that be sufficient?'

'For the present, but one day I may have to sell the settlement too. Of course, in the long run I may have to get rid of the lot, but the more land I sell, the smaller the harvests I'll get and the fewer men I'll be able to employ. Sometimes I wake in a panic thinking I'll never finish.'

'You will, my son. The Holy One will not fail you. We will pray for you and Zillah.'

The sale went through soon after harvest, but to Noah's surprise Zillah took the news calmly.

'I'm not surprised. I knew you'd ruin us eventually, you old fool! I suppose I should be thankful we still have the settlement – for now.'

'But I had to do it if I'm going to build the ark...'

'The ark! That's all you care about!'

'But you know why – I thought you shared my vision.'

'I suppose so, but it's so long ago. I'm afraid that soon we'll be back in a tent slaving our guts out working for our neighbours!'

'But don't you see? I'm selling the estate so we can get a whole new world in exchange!'

She pushed him out of the way and hurried outside sobbing. Everything he said made things worse.

17

The ark seemed to grow by itself. The two lower decks with their storage facilities were complete and the men were working on the top level. Then Shem married Ishtar.

'She's a lively girl,' Noah remarked to Zillah, 'and very pretty too.'

'That's all you men think of! I think she's nothing but trouble. Shem was mad to fall for her.'

As Zillah bustled away, Noah sat thinking.

'It's a pity they named her after a goddess. It's odd that's the first conversation I've had with Zillah for weeks, but we'll have to talk seriously soon. I've used up my gold and I'll have to sell the settlement.'

But as soon as tried to explain his plans, she interrupted.

'I know exactly what you're going to say. You're going to sell the settlement.'

'How did you know?'

'I've watched you trying to pluck up the courage to tell me you're going to sell the roof over my head! Don't mind us so long as you have your wretched boat.'

'But I've still got land and I've found just the place for our new home.'

'Next to the ark, I suppose!'

'Well, yes.'

'I won't leave here till I'm carried out in a shroud!'

Noah clenched his fists in frustration.

'You'll be leaving within the month. I'm selling most of the estate and that's it!'

'Go and build your new house – but don't expect me to live in it.'

For the next few weeks she took to her bed until the moment came to walk out of the door for the last time. Noah looked back longingly, but she stared straight ahead as if her face was carved out of rock.

The latest sale aroused considerable interest in the Great Valley. Most people saw it a sign of Noah's descent into madness.

One day, three strangers came in and walked up to the very pillar where Noah was standing.

'Good bit of timber – he knows where to get it!'

'There's some beautiful stuff here, and nicely finished.'

'They say he's got some bronze tools too. They'll be worth getting hold of.'

Noah stared in amazement.

'I may be old, but I'm not dead and I'm not stupid! Get out!'

But even worse was when two Nephilim appeared.

They were huge arrogant men, wandering around with their bodyguards as if they owned the place.

Noah felt as if his bowels had turned to ice.

Then one spoke.

'An interesting little boat you've got here; we've taken quite a fancy to it. We'll be happy to take it off your hands and give you a little gold for your old age!'

Then Noah found his voice.

'I'm not selling. The Holy One has told me to build this ark so we can escape the flood that's coming.'

The man laughed, then his eyes bulged. 'Not a very sensible answer! People who say no to us usually regret it – if we give them time!'

Then a divine rage came on Noah and to his amazement he heard himself shouting.

'I'm not giving you anything. Leave my property immediately!'

The man lurched forward, hands outstretched, veins standing out on his forehead. Then suddenly his arms dropped and he turned to his companion. 'Perhaps we should leave; we're not welcome here.'

Then, without warning, he roared so loudly the deck shook.

'You won't get away with this, old man! We'll be back and by the time we've finished with you there won't be any trace of your precious boat!'

They swaggered down the ramp, their bodyguards scurrying after them. But despite his fear, Noah knew they would never return.

Reu left a week later; he had never forgiven Noah for giving Ehud responsibility for the ark.

'Are you sure you won't change your mind?' Noah pleaded. 'You're part of the family.'

'No, I fancy going upriver where I can be my own boss.'

'But I'm keeping room for you and your family in the ark when the flood comes.'

'Master, I'm not coming back. Give it to someone who believes in all that stuff.'

'I've failed Reu,' Noah confessed to Shem later. 'I couldn't convince him the flood's coming.'

'I'm afraid that's his decision.'

'But it's getting me down. Nobody's taking me seriously and I've lost a lot of good men lately.'

'Don't worry, Father. The rest are very thankful for a job. They'd be hard put to find a better master.'

'But sometimes when I think what this has done to everybody, especially to your mother, I wonder if I've imagined it all.'

'You, Father? You've got doubts? But you're the one who keeps us going!'

'I'm sorry, I shouldn't have said that. But I don't know why the Holy One chose me of all people.'

'Because you're the only man capable of doing it, and I'm proud of you! People laugh about the ark but they're amazed at what you've done.'

'If only they believed my warnings about the flood, it would be worth it.'

The walls were complete, leaving a gap at the top for light and air. Now Ham had made a model of the roof.

'It'll be pitched, with a slope at each end. We'll thatch it with reeds, rope them down and cover it in pitch. We're expecting stronger winds and heavier rain than any we've known.'

The roof timbers were the longest they had used and were hoisted using a double team of oxen. They had some difficulty finding men with the courage to work at that height, but one day, to his surprise, Ham saw Noah climbing the ladder.

'Be careful, Dad. There's not much to hang on to!'

'I want to see for myself that they're doing a good job. If there're any gaps it'll be awful inside when the rain falls.'

He had never been so high before. A wind was blowing and everything rocked gently. He glanced down and saw the men looking like children and in panic grabbed one of the trusses, only to feel it move. Then, when he felt calmer, he backed towards the ladder, looking upwards and feeling with his foot for the top rung. But when he saw Ham afterwards he said, 'You'd better get used to seeing me climbing ladders; I'll keep checking the roof till it's done!'

They finished in autumn, and Noah gave a feast to the men. But he was sad, remembering Reu and the other men he had failed to persuade.

That evening some men arrived looking for him.

'Your grandfather Methuselah sent us,' their leader explained. 'Your father is very ill and wants to see you as soon as possible.'

'Don't die yet,' he muttered to himself. 'There are so many things I want to say.'

As they left the forest at the end of the journey, clouds were massing in the west and it was snowing before they reached the gatehouse. Methuselah met them there.

'Thank you for coming so quickly! I do not think he will live till morning so I have made my farewell.'

They had put Lamech in his favourite room facing the setting sun. But now the only light came from a lamp. He had always seemed small, but now he looked like a child. Noah took his hand; it felt icy despite a peat fire in the room and shawls wrapped around him. Then he called in a faint voice.

'Son, you are here at last. I can go in peace. Be strong; it will not be long now. I only wish I could have seen your new world.'

Then Noah was alone. He rose and closed his father's eyes.

18

They buried him in the courtyard where he used to sit in the sun.

Methuselah gave the orders. 'Dig his grave deep so his body is not washed away by the flood.'

Noah had fresh tears as he realised how firmly the old ones had believed in his vision. Afterwards he sat with his grandfather, thinking just how lonely he would be now.

Eventually Methuselah spoke. 'I have heard many things in my life, but nothing as important as the work the Holy One has given you to do. Your father and I prayed for you continually.'

'Thank you, Grandfather. I wish I could show you the ark.'

'I will never leave here again, but from what you have told me, it is as familiar as those mountains over there.'

Then he spoke again. 'When I die, promise me you will close my eyes as you did for my son.'

Noah wanted to stay longer, but the track was getting thick with snow and his men dragged him away. But all he could think of was his grandfather's loneliness.

There was still much to do and so little gold left. Then he remembered Heth, a young man who farmed next to his estate. They were chatting one day when Noah made a suggestion.

'Are you interested in doing a deal?'

'What have you got in mind?'

'Would you like to buy some of my land?'

'You're not selling any more, are you?'

'Perhaps, if I get a good offer. Come over and we'll discuss it.'

After showing him the estate, Noah took him to the ark.

'I want to keep this and a field or two. Otherwise, I'll let the rest go.'

'But you'll hardly have enough to support your family.'

'Maybe, but I've got to finish my work.'

'If you don't mind me asking, when will your flood happen?'

'Perhaps five years from now or a bit less.'

Afterwards Heth puzzled over this bizarre conversation. 'Noah's such a sensible chap. If it wasn't for his obsession, he'd be an ideal neighbour. I suppose I shouldn't take advantage of someone who's mad, but chances like this don't often come my way.'

Next day he made an offer.

'Noah, why don't I buy everything you've got, including the ark. I'll give you a fair price but wouldn't take possession for five years.'

'What would I do in the meantime?'

'Carry on as usual.'

'What, grow crops and harvest them?'

'Exactly! After five years, everything becomes mine except your last harvest.' Then he smiled. 'And if there is a flood I hope you'll save me a place in your ark!'

'I'd want you to come with us anyway.'

For three days Noah fasted and called on the Holy One. Then he visited Heth.

'I accept your offer, but can we keep it secret?'

'Are you trying to hide this from Zillah?'

'Yes, that's my problem.'

A priest of Marduk witnessed the contract in the approved manner and now Noah had the gold he needed to complete the ark and stock it. He felt guilty about Zillah and he still had doubts: if he was wrong about the flood or its timing he would lose everything.

He was on the top deck with Ham, Kenan and Enosh. It was an enormous space, lit only by sunlight coming through the door and the space above the walls.

'We'll live down that end, with separate rooms for each family and a space where we'll meet together. There'll be accommodation for all of you and anyone who wants to join us.'

Enosh and Kenan shifted uneasily but Noah was too busy to notice.

'The rest of the space is for our animals. The flood will drown everything except fish, so we'll take breeding pairs of everything with us to restock the land once the waters go down.'

Ehud interrupted. 'Cattle, sheep, that sort of thing?'

'Yes – and everything else that breathes: birds, snakes, wolves, vultures and scorpions.'

'But how will you manage with all those unclean animals and birds around?'

'They'll all be in pens or cages.'

'And where will you get them all?'

'We have the oxen, sheep and goats already, but as for the rest, the Holy One will find them for us.'

Ham was looking upwards.

'I suggest we build a walkway up there under the window space so we can keep watch, and be able to throw out all the dung and old bedding.'

'Then there'll be all the bilge water,' Noah added.

'Why? Will the ark leak?' Ehud asked.

'It will a little, and there may be spray and waves coming over the top.'

'But we're so high up.'

'Once it's loaded, the ark will float quite deep. But in any case we'll fit shutters all round to keep out the worst of the weather.'

'Why are there bricks and clay in the middle?' Kenan asked.

'For a fireplace so we can cook and dry our clothes. It shouldn't get swamped there, but we'll have to keep an eye open for sparks. The smoke will go straight up into the roof, and we'll store wood and charcoal up there.'

'How will you feed the animals?'

'We have those storage bins with things like grain, beans and pulses, and hay and sawdust for bedding.'

'But will the wolves and vultures eat beans?'

Ham broke in. 'We could try them on dried fish. A lot of folk in the city eat it, and there are always fishermen by the river.'

Next day Noah took a party down there. Three men were in the shallows throwing nets, muscles rippling over their backs.

'I wouldn't like to argue with them!' Ham whispered.

Just then the tallest turned around to see a dozen armed men behind him.

'Trouble!' he shouted.

The men threw down their nets and within seconds were standing defiantly pointing barbed fish spears.

'Put your weapons down!' Noah shouted to his men, and then he walked forward holding his arms out. 'I'm sorry to startle you, but I wanted to see what you're doing.'

'Haven't you seen men fishing before?'

'Yes. But I want to learn how to do it.'

'Come on, don't make fools of us. We've got work to do! And take your men away. They make me nervous.'

It took some time to pacify him, but a bag of grain helped. Then the three men started fishing again and by noon had filled their baskets and were bundling up their nets.

'Satisfied? Anything else we can do for you?'

'Yes! I'd like to see how you deal with the fish.'

'Come along, if you must. But I don't want no trouble or it won't be just fish we'll be gutting!'

The three fishermen lifted their huge baskets and set off so quickly Noah could hardly keep up. They stopped by an untidy huddle of huts where the smell of rotting fish was overpowering.

Some women appeared and knelt by the baskets and Noah marvelled at how quickly they gutted each fish. Then an older woman tossed one at him.

'Care for a chew, dearie? Do you a power of good!'

They all laughed, but Noah felt sick.

'Do you eat it like that?' he said at last.

'Ain't you heard of cooking? Or dried fish?'

The tall fisherman walked over. 'Come, I'll show you. By the way, the name's Shamash.'

They approached some wooden racks covered in what looked like grey rags, but Noah realised they were pieces of fish. Shamash picked one out and gave it to Noah. It felt like leather.

'What we can't sell we dry here. When it's hard like this it lasts a good time, particularly if you salt it.'

'Can you eat this?'

'No problem! Just soak it a bit to soften it and get rid of the salt and it cooks beautiful. Some folk feed their animals on it!'

'That's what I was going to ask! Do they really like it?'

'They'll eat it if they're hungry.'

'Well, I'll have a lot of animals to look after so I could put some work your way!'

19

Two weeks later, Shamash and his friends began fishing near the ark. Soon they had produced their first load of dried fish, but were running out of salt. The traders were charging so much for it that Noah decided to collect some himself, taking Shem and guided by Shamash.

They travelled downriver with the current, but after several days the pace slackened as they reached the delta. Then Shamash called a halt.

'This is the best place to stop since you can see people coming before they're too close. We can get to the sea and back in a day by reed boat. The locals will take us, they'll do anything for a bit of grain, but keep an eye on them. They'll slit your throat as soon as look at you!'

'Where do we find them?'

'Leave it to me.'

Noah left Shem with half the men to guard the raft and oxen while he and Shamash took the rest of the party. Soon they found themselves in a bewildering sequence of small channels flanked with tall reeds. It was swelteringly hot, but eventually they felt a cool breeze and the boat began rocking.

They had entered a huge expanse of water stretching as far as they could see. In the distance Noah saw another reed boat being successively lifted high on a wave then buried in a trough, and he had a vision of the ark fighting for survival on a rough sea without shores.

They landed on a beach backed by a row of sand dunes.

Shamash pointed to them. 'The salt works are just over the other side. But let me do the bargaining. I know what these men can get up to!'

Noah struggled up the slope, but at the top he was dazzled. Salt spread out below, shining like snow, and he could see men burnt black by the sun shovelling it into bags.

It took days to load the raft and Shamash was getting nervous. 'I've never known it this quiet. I reckon something's going to happen.'

Then, as they were loading the last of the salt, he saw a column of smoke upriver.

'Master, like I said, we've got trouble. Looks like that village is on fire.'

Noah breathed a prayer to the Holy One. 'Well, unless you know of another route, we'll have to pass that way.'

As they approached the spot, there were still clouds of smoke and piles of embers where the huts had stood. But there was no one around.

That evening Shamash said, 'We were really lucky today. I thought we were going to be next.' And he related some horror stories of ambushes, of rafts and men disappearing at full moon and of bodies floating in the river.

'Nothing like that's ever happened to us in all our trips to get timber and pitch,' Noah remarked.

'No rafts lost! That's incredible! You've got a powerful god looking after you!'

They returned home without further incident and resumed work. Soon the fishermen had filled several bins with fish and Noah called a halt. But Shamash was sorry to be leaving.

'I suppose we'll have to return to the city, though I doubt we'll find another stretch of river as good as this.'

'Well, there's always room for you in the ark when the flood comes.'

'Thanks, Master. But I'm not scared of a bit of water. I can swim or use my boat!'

There were three weddings that autumn. Ehud announced he was marrying Milcah from the village, although Zillah did not approve. 'He's not the marrying sort and she's much too young for him.'

Then Japheth found Naamah and Ham married Siduri. Zillah was very relieved. She had been worried the family had got a bad name since Noah began building the ark and was afraid they would not be able to find wives. But as the months went by there was no sign that any of her daughters-in-law were pregnant, and she began to think the family had been cursed. She even blamed Noah for allowing the girls to work in the fields during harvest.

'They'll never get pregnant if they're exhausted. If you hadn't sold all that land we'd still have enough men to do the work. And incidentally, with so little land left, why did you waste a whole field growing sunflowers?'

Noah sighed, 'We'll have a lot of birds in the ark.'

'I'll believe that when I see it.'

Nearly four years had gone by since Noah had made his contract with Heth. Harvest was over, most storage bins were bulging and there were full racks of jars of olive oil and honey. However, he had left the water jars empty, intending to fill them at the last moment. Now his thoughts were turning to the animals he would take. Where would they come from?

Then one morning two small boys appeared, wearing muddy loincloths and clutching sacks.

'I'm Enkidu,' announced one, 'and this is my friend Ea. We've got something for you.'

'Well, Enkidu, let's see what you've got.'

When he saw the scorpion Noah jumped in alarm. 'Careful! That could really hurt you!'

'Yes, Master. But Dad said you wanted to collect lots of animals to put in your ark and so I reckoned we could help.'

'But who'd look after it?'

'Us! We'll come every day!'

'But this isn't a place for playing games.'

'We promise we'll be good!'

'I'll think about it. But could you find a mate for this scorpion?'

'Oh yes, and we can get you lots more – rats, mice, insects, snakes. We've got tons at home, but Mum wants us to throw them away.'

There was no stopping them. They were in every day, caring for their animals and bringing more. Enosh helped them make cages.

One day they brought a dove with a broken wing. Noah was delighted. 'Can you get me any more? I could use seven pairs if you can find them!'

It was time for Noah's journey to the hills. But Zillah was frightened.

'Must you go? Your grandfather won't miss you. Why not leave it till spring?'

'I must see how he is. I think it may be the last time.'

'Don't go! We've got so few men now and we're close to the road. I'm amazed we haven't been robbed already.'

'Well… perhaps I could hire extra men to cover while I'm away and I'll be as quick as possible.'

The harvest was so good that he was able to get 20 men to guard the family. He himself took six and Ham. It was a strange journey, so familiar, and yet he guessed he was making it for the last time.

When they reached the homestead they found only one man on duty.

'We're so glad you're here, Master. Your grandfather's had a fall and he can't get around.'

Methuselah tried to rise when he saw Noah, but the pain was too bad. However, he still insisted on a sacrifice next day, although they had to carry him up the hill on a litter.

Afterwards Noah spoke to Ham privately. 'There's just time to collect the last of our tools from the secret valley. We'll borrow two men from here to help carry them; I don't want ours to see what we're doing.'

It was years since they had been there. The hut roof had collapsed and it took some time to clear the debris. Then Ham levered up the stone covering the hiding place.

'There're about thirty items here, Dad, tools and a few bracelets – all bronze except for these three.'

He lifted out two iron axe heads and a bracelet, but they were covered in rust.

'Perhaps it'd be better to leave these behind in case any Cainites appear.'

20

As soon as they got back to the homestead, Noah knew something had happened to Methuselah.

They had put him into the room where Lamech had died. When he saw Noah, he said, 'I am going at last. The flood is almost on you; may the Holy One spare you. Do not forget the writings!'

They buried him near Lamech. Then Noah took Ham to an isolated barn and behind a loose stone found a bundle of clay tablets.

'Ham, these are very precious. They tell how the Holy One made the world and they also give the history of our ancestors. My father taught me to decipher them and made me promise to teach my children how to read them.'

That evening Noah invited the remaining servants to join him in the ark, but Adam shook his head.

'We're too old to come, but we'll be safe. No flood will reach us here.'

Noah woke at dawn, and as his men were getting ready to leave, he wandered off to pray.

Suddenly two young wolves bounded towards him. He recoiled in fear but they stopped within an arm's reach and sat watching him.

His men were shouting warnings and had grabbed their spears, but he called, 'Don't hurt them. They're my friends.'

The journey seemed unreal, like a story bards recite around a fire. The men were sweating under their extra loads, while the wolves trotted behind them like tame sheep. Then two young bears appeared and joined the procession, followed by two lion cubs.

Noah pinched himself, but he was not dreaming. These animals were behaving like those he had seen in his vision of Eden and he realised the Holy One had sent them.

The animals vanished when they stopped for the night, but reappeared next morning as they set out, and when they reached the ark they waited for Noah to lead them to their pens.

Ehud was amazed. 'In Marduk's name, Master, how did you tame them?'

'I did nothing. The Holy One sent them and they're going to live in the ark. Go and catch some fish so we don't need to open our stores yet.'

Next day Ham hung a long trough outside the window below the eaves. 'This is for when it rains, Dad,' he explained. 'It'll catch water from the roof and I've fitted a spout so we can fill the water jars.'

'But we'll use water from the well.'

Ham shrugged. 'It tastes better when it's fresh.'

That night Noah dreamed he saw the black cloud spreading over the western hills and a voice saying, 'The seventeenth day of the second month.'

He woke in a panic. 'It's only a week till the flood starts. We must move into the ark immediately!'

But would Zillah come? She hated the place and he wondered if he would have to drag her in by her hair! However, to his surprise, she smiled.

'Do you really think I'll stay outside? I don't intend to drown. And anyway our home now belongs to Heth.'

He stared in amazement. 'You know about our agreement?'

'Of course I do! You can't hide a thing like that from your own wife. I wish you'd had the courage to tell me yourself!'

'I though you'd be furious.'

'I was, until I had another dream about the flood and I knew you were right. But we'd better start moving if we're going in there today.'

His sons were happy to join them, but their wives were reluctant. Shem's partner Ishtar was particularly upset. Her family thought Noah was mad and were trying to talk her out of it.

Meanwhile, Noah ordered Ehud to move the domestic animals into the ark.

'A pair of each kind, Master?'

'Yes, but for the sheep, goats and cattle I want seven pairs, so we'll have enough to breed from and offer sacrifices. Choose the best and give the rest away.'

'I might take some off your hands, Master.'

'But I thought you were coming with us?'

'Well, I need to talk to Milcah. But there's a family wedding next week and I'd like to deal with that first.'

'But the flood will have started by then.'

'I'll think about it, Master. Maybe I'll choose a room and leave my stuff in it.'

Then Noah asked Enosh.

'Much obliged, Master. But I don't fancy being cooped up with all them wild animals. If it does start to rain, leave the door open for me.'

Then he tried Kenan.

'I know it's right for you, but, well... if it does look like rain, I may drop by then.'

Then Heth appeared.

'I hear you're moving into the ark, so you won't need your house any more. I don't want to rush you, but my wife's very keen on living there. I know our agreement's got a little time to run, but would you mind if she came across this afternoon for a look?'

'That's fine. But have you thought any more about my invitation to join us in the ark?'

'Well, everyone admires you for what you have done. What an achievement! But this business of a flood...'

'Don't you believe it?'

'I don't want to hurt your feelings... But if I were to move in, there would be a lot of talk from the men I'm making deals with and I'm a very busy man...'

The next few days were hectic. Ehud selected the best young specimens from Noah's livestock to take in the ark and found to his utter amazement that they were willing to be penned next to the wolves, bears and lions.

Birds and bats kept appearing. On one morning alone Noah found pairs of vultures, ravens, eagles, owls, quail, sparrows and partridges waiting patiently to be admitted. There was also a steady stream of wild animals: foxes, jackals, hyenas, gazelles, badgers, otters, hippopotami and even crocodiles, and the men made bets on what would arrive next, although they got out of the way when two leopards appeared!

Crowds of people came. Most thought it a huge joke, laughing as they milled around the cradle, the children playing make-believe games about taming monsters. Noah kept warning them that they would be dead within a week if they did not come in, but he had no response and became very discouraged.

'What's wrong with everyone? They've seen me build the ark, and they must know that was a miracle; I could only do it because the Holy One helped me. And I'd have thought that seeing all these animals living happily together might tell them something. There's been nothing like this since Eden. But what a tragedy! Wild animals and birds have the sense to come for shelter while the very men who built the ark don't understand a thing! They come in each day to feed and muck out the animals, but it's just a job and they're already wondering what to do when they've finished here!'

But he was encouraged by Enkidu and Ea. He really liked them and was hoping to take them with him. Then one afternoon he heard shouting.

Two women were arguing with Ham by the ark, but when he approached they set about him.

'Where are our sons? What have you done with them?'

'Dad,' Ham explained, 'these are the mothers of Enkidu and Ea come to look for them.'

'That's right! We've come to take them home – right now!'

'I saw them going onto the top deck. As you know, they come in every day to look after the insects and animals they've given me.'

'We know no such thing! We had no idea where they were slinking off to. But it's stopping right now!'

'But they've been a great help.'

'What have you been filling their heads with, you old fool? All that blithering nonsense about a flood and building a boat – you're not fit to be alive!'

They pushed past him, shouting for their sons; then emerged dragging them behind them. As they left, the setting sun lit halos round the boys' heads. Noah never saw them again.

Now everything was complete except for filling the water jars. The purest supply was an old well near the boundary, but despite a hard day's work only half the jars had been filled.

'We can finish this off tomorrow,' Noah shouted to Ehud.

'Sorry, Master. Young Marduk is getting married, none of us will be here, but we'll try to look in first thing to give a hand with the animals.'

Noah summoned his sons. 'I hope none of you are planning to go to that wedding. We've got to fill the rest of the water jars. I wish we'd done it last week. But while you're here, let's check that the door closes all right.'

'Don't worry, Dad. It worked fine last time.'

'But it's been lying open for months, with everyone walking over it. Put a rope over that beam and we'll use the oxen to pull it up from inside.'

Noah stood on the cradle as the door was raised.

A muffled voice came from inside. 'Is it up as far as it'll go?'

'Yes! The top's right against the lintel.'

'But there's a huge gap either side. I could get my head between it and the framework. It must have warped.'

'Can you get the locking bars to fit?'

'Not a hope. The door would need to come in at least a metre.'

They lowered the door gently onto the ground.

'Well, we'll have to take the whole door apart and straighten it,' remarked Ham.

Noah groaned. 'That would take weeks and the flood's starting tomorrow!'

'Then you'd better ask the Holy One for a delay!'

21

When Noah woke it seemed a normal autumn day, but the animals were subdued.

The men were late, bleary-eyed after a party, and Noah stared at them in dreadful fascination, knowing he would never see them again.

They barely listened to his usual warning.

'Sorry! Can't stop,' Ehud muttered as he finished feeding the animals. 'Milcah will kill me!'

Noah turned to hide his tears. Then Ham shouted.

'We've got to do something about this door!'

They tried putting on more pitch and trimming the wood but nothing worked. Then around mid-morning Noah saw the terrible cloud and knew his nightmare was coming true.

Reu was walking with Ki across the clearing where Noah had felled his trees.

Suddenly Ki pointed. 'Look there! We're in for a hell of a storm!'

But a horrible certainty was gripping Reu.

'I'm a fool. I had my chance and I threw it away.'

Then he turned to Ki. 'Remember when we were felling trees? Noah was building a huge boat with them to save our lives when the flood came. Well it's just starting and I'm on this godforsaken hillside instead of safe and snug inside. I'm going to die! We all are!'

Ki grabbed his arm. 'Well, let's sacrifice to Enlil.'

'No, a storm god can't help us. The Holy One himself is doing this!'

He hurried to his hut, where he kept a jar of poppy juice. Just one mouthful would ease the worst pain and give the sufferer sleep, but he drank the lot.

Noah made a quick check. The whole family was there apart from Ishtar.

Shem explained. 'She's gone to the village to help her mother. It's Marduk's wedding.'

'I told you not to let her out of the ark! We must get her back now!'

'She won't come until after the wedding.'

Noah seized his arm. 'Look at that cloud! The flood's starting!'

Shem's mouth dropped open.

'Come on! And the rest of you get that door fixed while we're away.'

A chill wind was blowing, but terror drove them on. As they reached her parents' home Shem paused at the door but Noah barged in and found Ishtar dressing.

'Get out! How dare you! I might have been stark naked!'

'Come back with us now! The flood's starting!'

'Don't be so stupid! I'm off to the...'

But Noah had thrown her over his shoulder. She screamed, drumming her fists against his back. Then he saw her mother bearing down.

'Rape! He's raping our daughter!'

Noah had the strength of insanity. Brushing her aside he lurched across the courtyard.

'Shem! Come on! And the rest of you too, or you'll drown!'

Noah carried Ishtar as far as the estate boundary then he gasped.

'Take her, Shem. I'm done!'

Somehow they got back to the ark. The door was still open and Ham was standing there.

'Is everyone here?'

'Yes, Dad.'

'So get that door closed!'

'But we can't! We've tried everything.'

'We'll drown like rats!'

Noah stared outside with a deep sense of foreboding. There was an eerie glow in the sky, with flashes of lightning. And the wind was getting stronger.

Then he saw the whirlwind. A great black funnel of cloud visible beyond the village, twisting and turning violently, rumbling and crackling like some huge animal eating its way towards them. He watched in horror as it reached a row of trees by the village. Unbelievably, they were swept up into the sky. For a moment he saw the trunks spinning around the funnel like straws. Then they were gone.

At that moment Ishtar pushed past him, running towards the door, but she stumbled and he caught her. She scratched his face like a wildcat until Shem manhandled her back inside. Then she collapsed.

The funnel of cloud was almost on them. The roof of the rope store lifted off in one piece and flew into the cloud. The noise was indescribable and Noah clutched a pillar to save himself as the whirling mass came closer.

Then the door leaped up, smashing against the frame. Something struck his shoulder; then it was completely dark. The roar of the whirlwind was muffled, and he heard Ishtar sobbing.

He fumbled his way up to the top floor where there was some daylight and climbed to the lookout position.

The ark seemed intact and the whirlwind was gone. Then Ham appeared with a lamp and they went back to the door to examine it. It was completely shut, with no daylight showing and pitch forced out all around the frame. Even the bars had dropped into their sockets and were locked solid. There was a pattering noise above them, which became a steady drumming.

Then Noah knew. The Holy One had shut them in before the rain began.

Ehud was enjoying the wedding but felt a little uneasy. Noah had tried so hard to stop him leaving that morning.

He stepped outside for some fresh air and saw the cloud covering half the sky, blotting out the sun.

Back inside some dancing girls were beginning their show.

'The flood's started!' he whispered to Kenan.

'Not now!' he hissed. A black-haired girl was shrugging off her robe, nice and slowly.

Ehud looked for Milcah and glimpsed her in a corner.

'The flood's started! We've got to get back to the ark!'

'You drunken beast! Lose yourself and take your dancing girl with you! I saw you eyeing her up and down!'

As he tried to grab her, she slapped his face and some men hustled him away.

'Drown if you must!' he yelled. 'I'm off to Noah!'

'Keep your Noah and his animals! I never want to see you again!'

As they shoved him outside, the whirlwind roared past. Then, as the noise died away, he started running for his life as the first drops of rain fell. Soon he was soaked to the skin, and could hardly see anything, but somehow he found the ark.

'They've shut the door,' he gasped, and running towards it began hammering with his fists.

Then he heard someone calling and could just make out Ham looking down at him.

'Sorry, Ehud. It's shut and we can't open it!'

Ehud stared up at the wall glistening in the rain, but there was no way up – the scaffolding had been removed long before. Then he remembered a ladder they had used when cleaning bird droppings off the wall. It must be around somewhere.

Eventually he saw it floating below the cradle. Stripping off his precious new robe he jumped down and began dragging it up. A ladder this size needed three men to carry it, but somehow he got it up single-handed. The end had snapped off, but it would have to do. He lifted the broken end and began levering it up until it was resting against the wall of the ark. It was just too short; ending about four paces below the window space. If he could get up there he might be able to clamber in, but there was nothing to hold the ladder in position and he wasted precious moments hunting for a rope.

'I'll have to balance somehow.'

But the ladder stirred with his first step and rain was sluicing down from the roof, so it was like climbing through a waterfall. He had never gone so slowly, setting his foot softly on each rung before trusting his full weight, freezing with each slight tremor.

At last he was at the top. Here the eaves sheltered him from the worst of the water, but the wall seemed to be pushing him backwards. The last rung was hard up against the wood; he could hardly get his fingers round it, but if he was to reach the window he would have to stand on it. Then he saw Ham.

'Drop me a rope! I can't hang on much longer!'

Ham seemed to be gone for ever. Ehud's legs were trembling under the strain and the wind had strengthened, buffeting him with spray.

'This is all I can find.'

Ham dropped a rope down, the ragged end hanging just out of reach to the right.

He twitched it along, and Ehud stretched out a hand to touch it. Then the ladder lurched and he made a grab, but his fingers slipped on the wet strands. The ladder pitched sideways. He caught a glimpse of the swirling waters far below. Then he fell, smashing down onto the cradle. His fingers scrabbled on the wet wood then pain engulfed him and he slipped off. The cold water revived him and he grabbed a large log jammed between the brickwork piers.

'Hang on!' he told himself. 'Ham knows I'm here and he'll find a way of rescuing me.'

But the current shifted his log and it floated under the ark. Somewhere underneath the timbers he had helped lay, he found himself in utter darkness with his head jammed in a pocket of air. Then slowly it filled with water.

22

One moment Noah was standing by the door, the next he woke up in his cabin.

'He's opened his eyes!'

Zillah was smiling down at him, then he realised she was shouting. His ears were filled with a thudding sound, and it took a moment to realise it was rain lashing the roof.

'What happened?'

'You fainted. You're too old to go around carrying your daughter-in-law. You've got to rest!'

'But there's so much to do!'

'Stay there – don't move!'

He waited until she left, then sat up. He could see spray coming through the window space, soaking the floor. Then he pulled himself upright despite feeling dizzy.

'Ham, Shem, Japheth, get that shuttering up over the windows. Then the men can...'

But there were no men, and he felt horrified as he imagined them dying in that terrible rain. He had tried so hard to warn them, but the only person he had saved was Ishtar.

'Stupid man! I told you to rest!'

Zillah had returned, but even as she spoke, they felt the ark stir beneath them and there was a scraping noise.

'What's that?' Zillah asked.

'We're starting to float.'

The deck was rocking and there was a chorus of creaks.

'But we're falling apart!'

'That's nothing to worry about. All new rafts sound like that before the wood swells and the ropes tighten.'

But he silently prayed, 'Holy One, may every rope hold!'

Kenan left the wedding soon after Ehud. He had had second thoughts and decided to pick up some stuff then go over to the ark. But the rain was so relentless he could hardly find the way to his hut where the floor was covered in water. Grabbing some clothes as they floated past, he set out again.

The path was knee-deep by now, and once he went in above his waist. Then he glimpsed the lookout tree by the estate boundary. He should be able to see the ark from here, but the mist hid it. By now the water was chest-deep and he began swimming until he struck his knee on something hard. He could feel a long piece of wood which was fastened to something. He pulled himself along until he felt some bricks and realised he was on the cradle.

'The ark's gone!' he shouted. 'I'm too late! I must get back to the wedding; someone will know what to do.'

He began swimming again, but the cold was seeping through him and it seemed more sensible to stop and go to sleep...

Noah felt a hand on his sleeve. Ishtar was smiling at him.

'I'm sorry, Father, but I've been silly. Yesterday I washed my blue cloak and put it on the bushes to dry. I forgot all about it, but if you could just open the door it won't take a moment to fetch it.'

He looked at her in amazement. 'We can't open the door! We're afloat!'

'But that cloak's special. Shem gave it to me! And we must let my family in!'

'I'm sorry, it's too late.'

'But what's going to happen to them?'

He paused. 'I'm very sorry, my dear. They're going to die.'

One of the dancing girls was sitting on Enosh's knee while he fed her grapes. Then the bridegroom gave a toast. 'To Noah and his voyage!'

There was a chorus of cheers.

'He's got the right weather for it.'

'Why don't we join him?'

The men had difficulty finding the door, and once they felt the rain they hurried back inside. As they were drinking another toast there was a surge of water, and the women scrambled on the benches to keep their robes dry. Enosh tried to catch his girl, but she evaded him.

The party was over. He waded to the door and found a river outside tearing at the mud brick wall of the building. Its current picked him up and swept him along. A moment later he slammed into a tree. Somehow he managed to grab a branch and pull himself up until he was sitting in a fork. Then he heard a rumble and saw the building collapse. He was alone, gazing down at the water swirling past. Then he sensed a dark shape approaching at terrifying speed and glimpsed great walls and a roof streaming with rain.

'It's the ark!' he screamed as it crushed him.

No one saw his death; it produced just one more thud as the ark struck various obstacles. Meanwhile, Ham was grieving for Ehud. He had seen his body crushed almost out of recognition as the ark floated away, and he blamed himself. 'I killed him. If only I'd found a decent bit of rope!'

Shem and Japheth roused him for a while to help lash down the shutters, but then he sank back into despair.

Heth was in the city making a deal with the priests. When the rain started they sheltered in a granary under the great tower. But soon a pool of water formed on the floor and the high priest went out to investigate.

He returned looking worried. 'I've never seen a flood like it; I think we'd better move upstairs. I'm sorry, Heth. You'll have to stay here tonight.'

But the water was climbing ever higher and finally they were forced outside onto the tower. There the rain was so heavy Heth felt he was being beaten by sticks.

'Maybe Noah knew a thing or two. I wish I was in his ark right now!'

Then the earthquake struck and he looked up to see the top of the tower falling directly onto him.

Noah was standing when the shock struck. He was thrown sideways and grabbed a pillar to save himself, jarring his shoulder in the process. The lamp had fallen over and in the darkness he felt he was falling into a bottomless pit. Then he heard a sound that he recognised from his nightmare and imagined the great wave curling high above them. In a moment he was thrown into the air before crashing down again and sliding helplessly until he came up against something solid.

He lay motionless, wondering if he was dead. Then he saw a lamp flickering.

Shamash had taken Noah seriously and stocked up his boat. He even felt pleased when it started raining.

'Clever of the old man to guess this was coming. But I'd rather be in a proper boat than stuck in his box.'

As they pushed off, he shouted to his wife, 'I've never seen the river like this. Keep an eye open for any rubbish that's coming down. A tree trunk would finish us off!'

But when the earthquake struck the boat grounded on the riverbed, then capsized as the water roared back. Somehow they got it back upright, but the food and water had gone and they started bailing with anything they could find.

Then in the distance Shamash heard a deep roar. He watched helplessly as the huge wave crashed down on them.

'Good! We're all safe.' Somehow Ham had managed to light a lamp and had gathered everyone together. 'There's bread here and a water jar.'

They all drank but no one felt hungry.

Ishtar seemed very agitated. 'We must sacrifice to Enlil or he'll kill us all!'

'No!' Noah shouted. 'This is the Holy One's doing. He'll protect us.'

'Do you think you could get a fire going?' Zillah asked. 'I'm freezing.'

Noah shook his head. 'Not tonight, I'm afraid. It's too dangerous, and if the ark jerks again like that the embers will go everywhere.'

'So what on earth happened just now?' Shem asked. 'Did we hit something?'

'I think it was an earthquake setting off a huge wave, like the one I used to dream about.'

'Will there be any more?'

'I don't know. But we can't afford to take chances. We'd better stay here together tonight and find something firm to tie ourselves onto.'

The night seemed endless and no one got much sleep. The rain hammered down and there were further shocks. Noah started retching but there was nothing left in his stomach.

Next morning Ham opened a shutter, but he could only see driving rain, mist and an endless succession of waves smashing against the hull.

The Great Valley was quickly overwhelmed. Most dwellings near the river were washed away before the earthquake struck. Then the sea erupted over the land, dousing even the sacred flames of the pitch lands. Some men reached the mountains but were driven back by torrents of water and mud. Forests were ripped out, leaving the hills bare.

The Cainites were the last to die. The priests continued their human sacrifices until the earthquake blocked the river gorge and their valley filled with water. Their slaves drowned in the blackness of the mines without ever knowing why.

23

Life in the ark was exhausting. There were no servants, and eight people had to do everything. There was permanent gloom and nothing was dry, with puddles everywhere and patches of mould on the walls.

The animals had livened up and the ark echoed to the bellowing of cattle, roaring of lions and howling of wolves. Only the bears were hibernating.

There were always animals to feed and muck out. Dirty bedding and dung was put in baskets and carried by a pair of yoked cows to the disposal point by the window space. Noah had got rid of his oxen since they could not breed.

Apart from the wood shavings, the fresh bedding was stored in the roof space and every time a bale was removed there were clouds of dust and soot. Soon everyone was coughing.

Another chore was filling the remaining water jars using Ham's trough.

'Do we really need this much?' Shem asked.

Noah nodded. 'I don't know how long we'll be here.'

'But why can't we use that water out there?'

'I suggest you try it!'

Shem lowered a jar on a rope, but when he tasted it he made a wry face. 'It's salty, like the sea that time we went down with Shamash.'

But worst of all was bailing out the bilges.

They groped down ramps in the darkness, guided only by a rope handrail while coaxing the cows along too. Despite the cold, the boys stripped down to their loincloths; it was all too easy to slop filthy liquid around while trying to fill a water skin carried by a restless cow.

'Will we ever get out?'

Zillah was in a black mood.

'Yes, eventually. But in the meantime we should be thankful we're still alive.'

'*Alive?* We're not alive! Your men used to call this place your coffin and they were right! It's the same shape, it's dark, it stinks and we're stuck here for ever. Then there're the girls.'

'What's wrong with them?'

'They've had enough too. They want out!'

'But there's nowhere to go! They've got to have patience!'

'You men don't understand what it's like living in this squalor. It's wet, it's cold, then there's that rain pounding, pounding, pounding, pounding on the roof and those filthy animals bellowing at us and making a mess!'

'You should be grateful you're safe!'

'I'd be better off drowned! Then I'd be at peace. I feel so shut in I could scream! Can't we find land somewhere? I want to feel the sun again.'

'You will, my dear. At least we have a future.'

'Some future, existing all by ourselves without any friends... Why did the Holy One have to kill everybody?'

'Because of their wickedness.'

'The Cainites were pretty bad, but what about all my friends? They didn't do any harm. Then there was Ea and Enkidu and also Ehud. He built half the ark and got drowned because he took a day off to go to a wedding!'

'I just don't know...'

'And another thing! Why did you let Shem marry Ishtar? She's nothing but trouble! All she does is sulk.'

After she had gone Noah murmured to himself.

'You don't know how I feel either! I'd give anything for a walk in the fresh air. I've had enough of this mess, to say nothing of fleas!' And he scratched his leg.

'We've only been here two weeks! It seems much longer. If only I could go and see the old ones once more!' In his mind he retraced the journey to the homestead.

Then he shook his head. 'The whole place must have been washed away. There's no way back. But I'd have loved to ask them why so many people died. Zillah's right. It does seem unfair, particularly for the children and babies. How could the Holy One do that?'

That night, as he lay on his damp straw, he tried to pray. But tiredness overtook him and he drifted off to sleep.

He found himself in the House of the Dead.

It was huge, stretching into the infinite distance. The spirits of the dead were there, each quite alone, trapped in their own alcove, unable to see the others.

He could not find his mother or Lamech and Methuselah, but he recognised many who had drowned in the flood. There was Ehud! He called out to him, but there was no response. He was talking to himself.

'If only I hadn't gone to that wedding, I could have been in the ark. It was plain crazy going up the ladder like that. I was always telling the men they should secure it properly first...'

Noah stood listening to his regrets and excuses. He kept repeating himself again and again like the refrain of a song.

Kenan was nearby. He was muttering too.

'It wasn't my fault! Nothing like that ever happened before. How was I to know that there was going to be a flood?'

Reu was standing silently, head down, while Heth was counting up something on his fingers.

Every kind of person was there – some sullen, others cursing their fate and the gods who had deserted them. There were even fire worshippers and shamans still trying to practise their abominable rites.

And there were women. Some were naked, still flaunting themselves, and next to them respectable housewives complained about their ruined homes. Their children were crying, begging to be allowed out to play.

There were some from the ill-fated wedding party. Marduk and his bride still waited to consummate their marriage, and her parents were afraid that the guests would blame them for the rain. There was Milcah, scowling with fury.

Then he came to the Cainites, still fingering their spears, and he shuddered. Would they guess he had stolen their secrets and leap out at him? And beside them were their slaves, slumped, despairing and naked.

Then the Holy One came.

Noah had seen him in his brightness in that vision of Eden. Now his glory had gone and he moved awkwardly as if he had been terribly injured. He hobbled slowly to each person, greeting them by name. Most ignored him, but some threw themselves at his feet. When he came to Ehud his muttering stopped and tears trickled down his cheeks. Noah clenched his fists, willing him to kneel, but the Holy One had moved on. Then, late as usual, Ehud tried to follow him.

Kenan was still pouring out his story, too busy to see who was in front of him. Then Noah watched as his servants and friends, one after the other, made their excuses and lost their opportunity. Sometimes the Holy One leaned forward to pick up a baby or cuddle children who ran out to him, and Noah was delighted to see Enkidu and Ea among them.

Then, to his amazement, he saw several Cainites following the Holy One, their faces beaming with joy, together with many of their slaves, stretching to their full height and striding out.

But most of the dead remained unmoved, some impassive, others cursing, threatening the Holy One with their spears or casting spells, while some of the women even tried to seduce him.

Finally, the Holy One approached Noah and suddenly he realised that his men had not rejected him after all but the one he worshipped.

The vast hall filled with light, his confusion and sadness were gone and he fell asleep.

24

Noah and Ham were looking at the spare cabins, intended for friends who had not joined them. Then Ham found a pile of clothing.

'Ehud left these behind to reserve his cabin. I might as well chuck them.'

Noah picked them up. 'There's still a lot of wear in them and it'll be a long time before we can make more. He won't need them again – more's the pity!'

'But, Dad! I killed him! If only I'd found a better rope!'

Then he broke down and Noah put an arm round his shoulders.

'It's not your fault. If he hadn't gone to that wedding he'd be here now!'

'That awful Milcah made him go!'

'If he hadn't married her it would have been someone else. He always put things off, and in any case I don't think he believed in the flood.'

'But what about the rest, Kenan, Enosh, Shamash and Heth? And Reu, of course. I nearly forgot him.'

'Well perhaps I could have said more, but I don't think any of them believed either, not even when the animals started arriving miraculously. They wouldn't risk making fools of themselves.'

'What about the people we never spoke to, and youngsters like Ea and Enkidu who couldn't choose for themselves?'

'The Holy One will look after them.'

'That's easy for you to say.'

'Well I had a dream last night. Perhaps I ought to tell you about it.'

Afterwards Ham looked puzzled. 'I can understand children believing in the Holy One, but surely not a Cainite!'

'I found that shocking too. They'd seemed as brutal as ever, but they changed once they saw him and started sobbing like babies, only somehow they were also bursting with joy.'

'What was it like when he spoke to you?'

'It was the best moment of my life. Nothing mattered when he was there!'

'But you said he'd been badly hurt. What had happened to him?'

'I don't know, but I think he must have been trying to help someone.'

'Will this rain ever stop?'

Noah looked at Shem in surprise. He normally said little.

'The Holy One told me it would last forty days.'

'I wouldn't mind that, but this awful darkness is getting me down. Those wretched lamps keep blowing

153

out, and we can't open the shutters because of the rain. Ishtar's in a dreadful state. She spends all day lying on her bed; she won't eat or even wash. She'll die if this goes on.'

Noah visited her later, but it took three attempts before she acknowledged him, then she screamed.

'Go away, you murderer! You killed my family! I wish I was dead too!'

'You mustn't die. There's so much to live for, a new world to bring your children up in!'

'Children! Don't talk to me about children! Shem's useless! He can't give me a baby. None of your sons can. We might as well be married to eunuchs!'

'But the Holy One's promised you some.'

'So that's what you want me for – so I can provide you with grandsons? Well, I'm sorry, I haven't obliged. And if your precious Holy One is any good he'd stop this stinking rain!'

One morning Noah woke and wondered what was different. He heard cattle stirring in their pens, water lapping, timbers creaking and the wind sighing.

'The rain's stopped!' he shouted, and rushed up the ladder to look outside.

The water was smooth, no longer ruffled by rain, and although mist hid the horizon, the heaviest of the clouds had lifted.

'Where are we, Father?'

Japheth had climbed up beside him.

'I don't know. I can't see anything I recognise.'

'Is it going to rain again?'

'Well, not like what we've just had. But would you please give me a hand opening the shutters? We'll all be better for light and fresh air.'

There was a new spirit in the ark, and Noah even heard Zillah singing.

Shem looked more cheerful too. 'Ishtar got up without being asked and had a wash. She's giving Siduri a hand with the birds.'

Meanwhile Ham was trying to catch fish. 'I've got some of those fishhooks Shamash gave me, and any I catch will feed the animals. That salt fish can't be too good for them.'

It was awkward fishing through the narrow window, and he had to give up when the wind freshened, but he got a good catch.

Noah was keeping a tally of the days by cutting notches in a pillar. Now he figured they were coming into spring, but it was unlike any he had known. The sun stayed hidden behind clouds, and a cold wind whistled around them. And the view was always the same, a circle of water surrounded by mist.

'We might be anywhere,' said Japheth miserably. 'Perhaps we'll keep floating till we run out of food.'

'No, the Holy One will find us just the right place to land. We've just got to be patient.'

'Patient! Patient! Mother swears that that's the only word you know!'

Noah was cutting his 148th notch on the pillar when Ham burst in.

'Quick! I've seen land!'

They hurried up the ladder, but all they saw was the usual wall of mist.

'I'm sure I didn't imagine it. It was as clear as you are – a huge mountain.'

Just then the mist thinned. 'Look, Dad! There it is!'

Some rugged cliffs appeared for a moment through the greyness.

'I hope we don't hit one of those! It would smash us up!'

But Noah looked calm. 'We'll have to trust the Holy One to keep us safe. He didn't tell me to provide oars, sails or a rudder so it's up to him.'

A fresh call that afternoon brought everyone onto the walkway to stare into the mist. Then there was a scraping noise and they felt the ark catch on something.

There were cries of, 'We've landed! Let's open the door!'

But to their disappointment the ark floated off again. It grounded several more times in the next two days but never settled. However, on the morning of the 150th day there was a big jolt.

'Here we go again!' Ham muttered, but Noah was more confident. 'I think we really have landed this time.'

Zillah was delighted. 'I can't wait to get my feet back onto solid earth!'

Noah was more cautious. 'I'm sorry, dear, but you'll have to wait till the water's gone.'

At midday Ham had another look. 'I'm sure it's going down. I've just seen some rocks I didn't notice before.'

Noah was staring at the floor. 'We're on a bit of a slope, but it's not too bad.'

Next day most of the water around them had gone, leaving an expanse of mud and pebbles. A stream ran down the hill nearby, but Zillah was not impressed. 'Noah, trust you to land us in a desert. There isn't a single tree!'

'But there won't be. The flood washed out everything. We must just hope there are still some seeds around to sprout.'

Anyway the girls and I want to get out. Would you open the door?'

Noah shook his head. 'I'm sorry, but you'll have to be—'

'Patient!' she broke in. 'Why can't you open it?'

'I think it's jammed solid and we'll have to break it down. But I can't do that till there's some grazing for the animals when we let them loose.'

'So you propose keeping us shut up in here till we go mad?'

'That's up to you!'

Then he turned to Ham. 'What have we got in the way of stores?'

'What's it matter, Dad? We'll soon be out of here!'

'As I was saying to your mother, it'll take longer than you imagine.'

'So how much food will we need?'

'Enough to see us through to harvest next year.'

'Why not plant some crops now?'

'It's too late; it wouldn't have time to ripen. That's why I want to check what we've got.'

They went down onto the bottom deck. It smelled very musty and a pool of water had formed at the lower end.

'That wasn't there when we bailed it out last week,' Ham protested.

'There may have been leaks when we landed. Anyway, let's look at the grain bins.'

'A lot of this is spoilt,' Japheth said, prodding it with a stick.

'Save as much as possible,' Noah replied. 'Throw the rest outside.'

'It would help if we could get someone inside to empty it from the top. I wonder if one of the women would do it, perhaps Naamah – she's the smallest.'

She clambered in and started filling baskets with the grain, which Japheth emptied into sacks. But soon she poked her head over the side.

'I'll have to come out. I feel sick.'

'Well, it can't be due to the ark moving around!'

'No. I've felt like this for days…'

25

The news of Naamah's pregnancy delighted Zillah. 'This is just what I've been waiting for!' Ham and Shem congratulated Japheth, although they felt envious, while Siduri and Ishtar were rather subdued.

One day Naamah was cleaning out the birds with Ishtar.

'These vultures really stink!' she complained.

'So is our mother-to-be a bit sensitive this morning?'

'I'm feeling sick – could you get me some water?'

'And what else would you fancy? Some nice fruit or flowers?'

'Ishtar, please! You know how it is—'

'No! I don't! It's all right for you, with a husband that's a man!'

Noah intervened to stop the fight but Naamah was very upset and lost her baby that evening.

Zillah was angry. 'That was the only grandchild we're likely to have! I wish I could get my hands round Ishtar's neck!'

'But she's bitterly disappointed too she's not had a baby.'

'Maybe. But I'll never—'

'Stop! She's Shem's wife and he won't be able to find another one! All our descendants will come from these three girls, so we've got to stick together. Whatever Ishtar's done, we must forgive her.'

Ham had thrown the spoiled grain over the side and there was a green mound where it had sprouted. But next to it was a pile of dung which smelled horrible, and there were flies everywhere.

'I never thought I'd miss the flood,' Noah remarked to Ham, 'but it did wash everything away!'

'I wish it would rain again, then we'd get fresh water. I'm sick of scraping muck out of the jars. And another thing, I'd love to know where we are.'

Everyone was wondering that as they gazed at the misty world outside. All they could see were cliffs and a valley in the distance.

'We've been lucky!' Ham remarked. 'We've landed on the one flat piece of ground.'

Noah nodded. 'Yes, I'm grateful to the Holy One for bringing us here safely.'

Then one morning Japheth called him up to the window. 'The sun! I've just seen it. I'd forgotten what it looked like!'

For a moment a pale disc showed through the clouds and Noah stared, willing it to stay.

The mist continued to rise, revealing huge crags and sheer precipices, then 74 days after they landed they saw the top of the mountain.

'I know where we are!' Noah shouted. 'I came here with Father when I was a boy. It's Ararat the great mountain! I'd know that peak anywhere.'

'So what's the country like round here?' Ham asked.

'Very good. It's warm in that valley and the soil's magnificent – you can grow anything. The only reason we didn't stay here was the idolatry. The locals worshipped the mountain and offered it human sacrifices. Even the Cainites thought twice about coming here.'

'But what about us? What happens if they attack us?'

'Haven't you forgotten? They all drowned in the flood!'

The sun grew stronger. It was warm and the ark began to dry out. The animals dozed in the afternoon while the family stood on the walkway, catching the breeze. One day Zillah found Naamah singing to herself.

'You sound happy.'

'Well, Mother, the sun makes all the difference, even if we can't walk outside yet.'

'But how are you feeling... really?'

'Well, sad. Losing the baby seemed like the end of everything – but maybe I'll have another. And I'm sorry I argued with Ishtar. She's miserable too.'

'I've seen you two talking.'

'We can't avoid each other, so we might as well be civil. We're both longing to get out of here away from the flies and smell. But why doesn't Father open the door?'

'He says he's waiting to hear from the Holy One.'

'Can't you persuade him?'

'I know him too well. He's stubborn and he's also frustrated.'

'Why?'

'He's never been happy unless he's got something to do and he's bored.'

Noah was trying to find out what it was like outside without having to open the door. He could lower someone on a rope, but memories of Ehud's fate were still fresh. Then he had an idea.

'I'll send out a bird and see what happens.'

His choice fell on a raven, pecking a putrid piece of fish that few other birds would touch.

'I'll try that one, it's pretty tough.'

The bird perched on his hand as he leaned over the top of the wall and gave it a push.

'Shoo! Go and see what you can find!'

It circled the ark then struck off towards the valley. He saw it several times winging its way overhead, but it never returned.

'That was a good sign wasn't it?' said Japheth. 'There must be food out there. Why don't we look?'

'Well, I've been having second thoughts. I don't think it was a good idea sending a raven.'

'What's wrong with that?'

'It'll eat anything, even a body left over from the flood. No, I should have tried a different bird that likes our food, maybe a dove. It should be safe; all the hawks are shut up in here!'

Noah launched it next day, although it was reluctant to leave. He kept an eye open for it but it was evening before it returned, looking exhausted.

'Poor little thing, you can't have found anywhere to settle.'

A week later, he tried again, but this time when it returned, it had something in its beak, an olive leaf, a beautiful silver-green with the sheen of new life.

'You've done well, little bird. I wonder where you found this?'

After another week he sent it out again, but it never returned.

26

A month dragged by. The mornings were cooler; it would soon be autumn.

'Won't you ever open the door?' Ham pleaded. 'How much more proof do you need? You saw that olive leaf – things are growing out there! The animals should be out and we should be ploughing, not moping about in here.'

'But we've—' Noah began.

'Don't say it! We've got to be patient! Until you get your sign from your Holy One!'

Noah rubbed his forehead in exasperation. 'I'm as desperate to get out as you are. But we can't rush things. If we let the animals out and there's no food for them, we'd be in an awful mess. I've been trying to see what it's like, but those rocks block the view. You'd need to be up on the roof to see over them.'

Ham looked interested. 'Why don't we get up there?'

'It's too dangerous. We'd fall off.'

Then Ham caught his father's arm. 'Why don't we make a hole in the roof? If we cut through the thatch by the ridge we could see everything. I'll fix up a ladder.'

Soon he was crouching under the roof, cutting the thatch away with a bronze knife and coughing because of all the soot and dust.

Before long, glimmers of light showed, then a large piece of thatch came away, almost knocking him off the ladder.

The brightness hurt like a blow and he shielded his face behind filthy hands. Then carefully he levered his head and shoulders through the hole. High above, the sky was unbelievably blue. White clouds drifted past, inviting him to travel with them. The sun was warm and the gentle breeze carried autumnal smells, reminding him of childhood and visits to great grandfather Methuselah.

Once back inside, he shouted, 'You can see right down into the valley. The water's gone and there's green everywhere.'

It was a terrifying climb for Noah, up makeshift ladders into claustrophobic darkness with one small patch of light to aim for, and his palms were wringing wet before he reached the top. He waited, trembling, for his eyes to get used to the light, then pushed his head cautiously through the hole. He had a moment of panic as he saw the ground so far below, then he scanned the view quickly before bracing himself for the descent.

'You're right about the valley. There's a lot of grass there,' he told Ham.

'So why don't we go there this afternoon?'

'It's no good. I still haven't heard from the Holy One.'

'But, Dad, what more can I do to persuade you?'

The next two weeks seemed never-ending. The family kept talking of their plans once they got out, and Noah could hardly look them in the eye. Even the animals seemed to accuse him of keeping them in.

He had cut his 365th notch – a whole year in the ark – and they were still trapped. Six days later, a gale brought the first flakes of snow, and that night he lay awake shivering as the wind moaned outside. Then the Holy One came.

There was brightness like the midday sun and a voice of thunder shaking the ark. Noah lay face-down in worship, sensing the figure in front of him as it commanded him to leave the ark and release every living creature.

A deep peace soaked through him. It had never been necessary to send out the raven or the dove or to make a hole in the roof. He had only needed to wait for the Holy One's time. Then he began worrying, had his family been disturbed by this visitation? Grabbing his robe he made a quick inspection, but everyone was asleep. The vision had been his alone.

To Noah's surprise, the cold weather had dampened the family's enthusiasm for leaving the ark, but he did get them to gather together.

'Is the Holy One opening the door for us?' Ham asked.

'No, I think it's up to us.'

But the locking bars were wedged so tightly that they had to break them with a hammer. Even then the door stayed shut until they picked up a large timber and used it as a battering ram.

The door fell with a tremendous crash, leaving them all cowering, overwhelmed by the sudden brightness, blinking like owls at midday.

Noah had dreamed of this moment so often, but now it seemed unreal. As he hurried outside, still shading his eyes, it felt as if someone else's feet were doing the walking.

Now, at last, he was walking through the long, clean, autumn grass, conscious that no man or animal had passed this way before, relishing the feel of firm ground and the smell of vegetation warmed by the sun.

Then he turned around, raising his head for the first time. It was a shock to see the familiar ark in this new setting, so insignificant against the mountains, his family looking like toys as they stood in the doorway.

'Typical! They keep complaining about being shut in, then when the door opens they're afraid to go out!'

Then a childhood memory surged back. He had climbed the hill to the stone of sacrifice when suddenly he realised he was on the edge of the world. The mountains he could see were uninhabited; there was not another living soul beyond him and in terror he ran home to his mother.

Now the only people still alive were his family. Every direction was the edge of the world now! The great emptiness began crushing him.

'Holy One, save me!'

Then, just as quickly as it had come, the fear left him. Instead a warm feeling began in his belly and engulfed him: all the years of toil and misunderstanding had been worthwhile. The Holy One had given him a new world, and once more he fell face-down in the rough grass in worship and thanksgiving.

As he returned, he shouted, 'Come out here! It's wonderful!'

They came out, cautiously at first, then they began shouting and playing like children, rolling over and over in the grass and turning somersaults. There was helpless laughter, a great crescendo of delight, releasing the horrors of the past year and making the hills ring.

Ham lay helpless, clutching his belly, and even Zillah was shaking uncontrollably. Noah began to chuckle then he roared out in joy.

But there was work to do.

In the daylight he could see the squalor of the ark. There was rubbish everywhere, pieces of fish alive with maggots, piles of dirty straw and toadstools sprouting from the walls. Worst of all was the stench, and he gagged after breathing the fresh air.

The family were still romping in the sunlight, but regretfully he called them together.

'Time to come in. We've got to let the animals go.'

They started with the birds, keeping the eagles and vultures until last. The day before, they had been moping, but now they were beating their wings as their cages were opened, blundering into their carers' faces in their eagerness to be gone. Soon the cages were empty apart from a few disconsolate pigeons and doves kept back for sacrifice.

The animals had come alive too, pacing impatiently around their cages and crowding the doors. They let the deer out first, then the sheep and cattle which sniffed the air before hurrying up the hill.

All the animals seemed to know what to do, but tears pricked Noah's eyes as he saw them leaving; he would never be this close to wolves, lions or bears again. The hippopotami left last of all, heading instinctively downhill towards water.

Now it was the turn of the insects and smaller animals, bringing back painful memories of Enkidu and Ea. Ham was carrying a large box.

'What have you got in that? Noah asked.

'Snakes.'

'I wouldn't take them outside now. They're very sluggish in the cold. Best leave them in here till next spring, and the same goes for the crocodiles and lizards. I hope the bears find somewhere to sleep through the winter.'

'They should be all right, they're nice and fat, but how will the lions and wolves manage?'

'We'll have to put out food for them till they're established; we've still got bins of that salted fish left. I don't want them killing the deer and sheep before they have a chance to breed.'

The sun was setting and a chill wind ruffled Noah's cloak, an omen of winter to come, and he prayed to the Holy One for protection during the cold months.

27

'I want to sacrifice to the Holy One to thank him for saving our lives,' Noah announced.

'Can't we leave that until we're sorted out?' Ham suggested.

'No, we need to do this first. I'm going to choose a ram to offer.'

'But we've so little stock. Can't we wait till we've bred more?'

'No, we must do it now while it's fresh in our minds.'

They built the altar of stones on a flat rock and put wood on top. To Ham's annoyance, Noah chose the pick of the flock. It came to him willingly, but he felt a sense of betrayal as it trotted beside him up the hill.

He had never sacrificed an animal before, although this brought back the dreadful memory of the woman he had stabbed. As he tickled the ram behind its ears, Japheth and Ham grabbed its horns and forced its head back and he drove his flint knife deep into its throat. Blood spurted out and he tried to catch it in a bowl before sprinkling the altar in the traditional manner. As his sons lifted the carcass onto the wood, he wiped his hands on some grass before lighting the pyre from his fire pot.

As he raised his hands in worship, he was conscious of Ishtar fidgeting; perhaps she remembered more spectacular rituals with robed priests and human victims. But suddenly the flames leapt high and the fire blazed like the sun.

As Noah rose stiffly from the ground, he saw the rest of the family lying round the altar. They rose eventually, their eyes glazed, but said nothing as they retuned to the ark.

Later Shem spoke to him. 'The Holy One came, didn't he, Father?'

'Yes, Shem, he did.'

'I've never been so frightened in my life. I thought I'd been struck by lightning!'

'He's like that. But did you hear what he said?'

'No just some thunder, then I think I passed out.'

'What about the others?'

'The same as me.'

'How strange. I heard him clearly. He accepted my sacrifice and said he wouldn't curse the land again. You remember he did it once because of Adam's sin, that's why it's so hard to grow anything.'

'But aren't we better than Adam?'

'No. In fact we're just as bad as the folk who drowned. We're evil through and through, and have been ever since we were children.'

'But he's given us another chance.'

'Yes, and he promised he'd never destroy all the living creatures again. And we'll have summer and winter again; and day and night as long as this world lasts. He even gave me a poem so I could remember it.

> *As long as the earth endures,*
> *seedtime and harvest,*
> *cold and heat,*
> *summer and winter,*
> *day and night*
> *will never cease.'*

'That's all very well, Father, but who's going to inherit this new world of yours?'

'Your children, of course.'

'But there aren't any children! I can't be a father and Ishtar treats me like a joke and it's the same with Siduri and Ham. They keep making eyes at Japheth, because he did manage to start Naamah off and they spend more time with each other than they do with us!'

'Let's go back to the altar today,' Noah announced next morning.

There was a shuffling of feet and Ham interrupted. 'We'd like to worship the Holy One sometime, but we've got a lot to do round here.'

'I know you were scared yesterday, but the Holy One's got more to tell us.'

'That was quite enough for me!' The whisper was just audible but Noah chose to ignore it.

'But we women don't want to come again,' Zillah objected. 'We were scared out of our wits.'

So Noah led just his sons back up the hill. It was cloudy, but as they reached the altar a shaft of sunlight lit it up.

They formed a self-conscious circle, gazing at the ashes, then Ham asked, 'So what are we doing here?'

'Waiting for the Holy One.'

The young men lapsed into sullen silence while Noah tried to meditate, but the conversation with Shem the day before haunted him.

'Of course, it's just as humiliating for my sons not being parents as for their wives,' he thought, 'but they find it harder to talk about.'

Then the light blazed again and he glimpsed his sons falling to their knees. The Holy One was telling them to have children and repopulate the world.

Noah was angry. Was the Holy One joking? Didn't he know of his sons' humiliation and the grief of their wives aching to hold a child and put it to the breast? But then he realised that this was not a promise or a pious hope, but a direct command. And he would help them to do it.

There was more. The terror of man would be put into every other living creature and they would be given to him to do with as he wanted. The friendship he had built up with the animals in the ark would soon be a memory.

Then came something shocking and obscene: the Holy One was giving him authority to eat animals as food.

'That's blasphemy!' Noah gasped. 'I've never eaten meat in my life. I've kept to fruit and seeds according to the ancient law.'

He sweated as he remembered killing that ram, but now was he was expected to rip the body to pieces and force quivering gobbets of flesh down his throat?

But there were restrictions. He must never eat meat with the blood still in it, since this was the life of the animal and, more important still, anyone or any animal that spilled human blood would be answerable to the Holy One. Then he heard another song.

> *Whoever sheds human blood,*
> *by human beings shall their blood be shed;*
> *for in the image of God*
> *has God made humanity.*

Of course! Cain spilled Abel's blood on the ground and the Holy One held him responsible. And the ram's blood he had sprinkled round the altar yesterday was a token of human blood.

He looked at his sons. Would they be killers too? But as if to reassure him, the Holy One repeated his command to multiply and fill the earth. And Noah murmured to himself, 'The Holy One loves them – and he's chosen them just as he chose me.'

'I had no idea he was like that,' Shem confided as he walked down the hill with Noah. 'I saw his fire and I heard him too. He's amazing, so much bigger than you can imagine and full of surprises. You never know what he'll do next!'

'So now you know what I've felt like all these years, being ordered to build the ark!'

'I see. But did he really mean that bit about us having children?'

No one wanted to continue living in the ark. It was dirty, smelled horrible and was very cold without a door. Instead they found a cave close by. The floor was covered in silt but it was dry and they brought wood from the ark to make windbreaks and as fuel for the fire. But Ishtar was nervous.

'Shouldn't we set a watch?'

'There's no one out there to harm us,' Noah reassured her.

'But what about the ghosts of the people who died? I can feel them all round me. I'm scared to go to sleep.'

'Don't worry. The Holy One's looking after us.'

But she kept as far away from the cave entrance as possible, and when she thought no one was looking she made the sign against the evil eye.

Noah was also disturbed with dreams of marching Cainites and waves crashing down. He awoke in the darkness and, pulling his cloak about him, walked to the entrance. The moon was full and he half-expected to see naked women writhing in a demonic dance.

The wind was sighing around the rocks, but there were no animal noises. 'I wonder if I'll ever stand in a forest again and hear birdsong,' he wondered.

He woke late. The women were tidying the cave and grinding corn while Ham was building an oven with bricks taken from the ark.

'I can't wait to bake proper bread again,' Zillah was saying. 'That fire in the ark was hopeless.'

Shem and Japheth were down by the ark laying out fish and hay for the animals and patting them affectionately. Then he noticed two black birds tearing at a fish.

'The ravens have found each other!' he exclaimed.

28

'We're lost!' Ham gasped.

He and Noah were watching a black cloud looking exactly like the one they had seen when the flood started.

His father was panicking too. 'Holy One, you're going to drown me in your new flood!'

Then he recalled his promise: 'I'll never destroy all living creatures again.'

Suddenly he was ashamed of speaking his fears aloud. Then he noticed Ham standing rigid with fear. He shook him. 'Ham – the Holy One isn't going to drown us!'

'But those clouds—'

'Just a storm. We'll always get rain.'

'But, Dad! We must get back to the ark!'

Then he began sobbing hysterically. 'We broke the door down! We'll never get it shut again! We'll drown!'

Noah slapped him across the mouth.

'Ham! This is only a passing storm. Find the others and bring them in here to shelter.'

Soon they were all standing by the entrance watching the rain blotting everything from view. But eventually it eased and the ark reappeared like a grey ghost. Then the sun came out, turning the wet rocks into jewels and making the mountains glow against the dark sky. Finally a rainbow appeared.

After a year of darkness starved of colour, they stared at it open-mouthed, utterly thrilled by its beauty and willing it to last for ever.

And the Holy One was there.

Noah fell to the ground as the voice rumbled around him. But when he stood up again, the others were still staring into the distance.

'So let's get this straight. When we see a rainbow we'll know it's something to do with the Holy One?'

It was evening and they were sitting around the fire.

'Yes, Ham. The rainbow's his special sign.'

'But we've seen them lots of times before.'

'Mum told me it was goddess Ishtar's jewels,' her namesake said quietly.

Noah twisted round. 'Enough of that talk!'

'Yes,' he continued, 'it isn't new, but it's got a new meaning. It's the sign of his covenant, his promise.'

'What's that?'

'He told me today there'd never be another great flood, and the rainbow will remind us of that. Otherwise we'll panic every time it rains.'

'How long will this promise last?'

'Till the end of time! And it's not just for us, but for every living creature. You remember Tiras?'

'What's he got to do with it?'

'Well, when he'd finished hunting, he'd put his bow away with the curved side up. It looked like that rainbow. The Holy One's been shooting at us but now he's put his bow down!'

A bitter wind was howling and Noah had called his sons together.

'Let's get as much stuff out of the ark as we can.'

'But haven't we got enough?'

'Not if we get deep snowdrifts. It'll be very difficult to carry anything then. In any case we'll have to bring the sheep and cattle in here and feed them, and we'll also need more fuel. I suggest you start breaking up empty food bins and partitions in the ark.'

'Are the wolves and lions coming in here too?'

'No, but we'll have to keep feeding them with dried fish.'

The three brothers found it hard work carrying heavy loads on their backs, but at least the exercise warmed them despite the cruel wind. Then at dusk Noah called Ham.

'I'm very sorry, but could you do me a special favour? I forgot to bring those writing tablets up here.'

'But I'm so tired. Can't it wait?'

'Not really. They're the most precious things I own and I must keep them safe.'

Ham groaned. 'All right, Dad, but let's make it quick!'

The next few months were grim, with everyone crammed in the front of the cave and the cattle and sheep at the back. They were restive after their few days of freedom.

Day blurred into day, a struggle to stay alive. Unless there was a blizzard, the men stumbled to the ark for more fodder, their hands cracked and bleeding. They built a snow wall to block out the worst of the north wind, then crouched over the fire catching fleeting moments of warmth, or huddled inside the cave, choking every time a strong gust swept smoke inside.

The stream had frozen, so they had to pile snow into water jars and drop in hot stones in order to melt it. Their food was still the stale provisions from the ark.

One afternoon, when the others were working outside, Ishtar found Noah slumped near the cave mouth.

'Are you all right, Father?' she asked, smiling.

He looked at her in surprise. Normally her face was very glum or angry.

'I suppose so, but I'm worried about Zillah. I don't know what to do about her. Everything I try seems to be wrong. I might as well not be here for any good I'm doing.'

Ishtar produced another rare smile. 'It's not your fault. She's very unhappy. It's been harder for her than the rest of us. She was really proud of her home, and now she's lost it. And she's missing her old friends.'

'But they've been dead over a year.'

'She still dreams about them almost every night. They used to drop in most days. She had a large platter of sweetmeats and they'd nibble them and have a good gossip.'

'I'll build her a proper house as soon as I can, and who knows, we may be able to find some honey. But I'm afraid there's nothing I can do about her friends.'

'Still, she'll enjoy being a grandmother.'

For a moment Noah did not realise what she had said, then he stared. It was the first time he had seen her blush.

'I'm going to have a baby. And perhaps I shouldn't say it, but so are Naamah and Siduri.'

29

'Look at the state of this place! What will the neighbours think?'

Zillah was getting frustrated with living in a cave. But Noah did not think this was the right time to remind her there were no neighbours. Instead, he remarked, 'Once we've finished the planting, I'll build you a new house.'

She snorted. 'I've heard that before!'

It was spring, the finest since the world began. The snow was melting, dark earth showed through and there were the first faint gurglings from the brook. The air was warm and sweet, flowers had appeared like magic, there was grazing for the animals and the ewes were heavy with young.

But their priority was sowing crops. They chose land near the ark where the grass grew strongest, with wheat close to the stream and millet on the poorer soil. They also planted beans and peas and sprinkled patches with herb seed. However, ploughing proved a challenge. They had no oxen and all the cows were in calf, so they had to use donkeys.

Meanwhile the women were struggling with the family's clothing. With no proper opportunity to wash since the flood began, their robes were thick with grease and vermin and in urgent need of repair. They spent days by the stream, pummelling the clothes over rocks or in a sheltered spot spinning woollen thread. Ham had promised them a loom and there would be babies to clothe come the autumn.

The men spent days deciding where to build their new home. Eventually they chose a spot near the ark; an outcrop of rocks protected it from avalanches and there was a dip in the ground.

'Let's dig this out further,' Noah suggested. 'It'll be a stable for the animals in winter.' We'll put the house on top and they'll keep us warm. But it took weeks to excavate the site, since under the soil there was a layer of rocks and each piece had to be prised free.

They built the walls of stone, setting each piece in carefully to get the best fit and filling the gaps with pebbles, straw and cow dung. They roofed it with timber taken from the ark and covered with turf.

They finished in late summer and Zillah examined it critically.

'It looks like one of the huts the servants lived in.'

Noah sighed. 'It's the best we can manage. At least you've got separate rooms.'

Then at last the harvest was gathered and it was time to celebrate. The new home was filled with the smell of baking using the fresh flour.

The family were impatiently eyeing warm bread and goat's cheese on the table when Noah picked up a loaf and broke it. 'The Holy One promised us harvests while the earth remained and here is the proof. This is a special day for us, a very special day indeed. So let us all thank him for his mercies to us.'

Ham was very excited. 'This food tastes wonderful – we can throw all our old stuff away.'

Noah held up his hand. 'Not so fast! I don't think we have enough new grain to see us through till our next harvest. We may be very grateful for that old stuff before we've finished!'

They feasted until it was time to light the lamps, then one by one they left to do their final chores. Only Ishtar and Shem were left, and she giggled as he patted her belly.

'Our first son!' he laughed. 'What do you think of your husband now?'

'I've met worse. Anyway I'm not looking for anyone else!'

She went into labour on a wild autumn day with a gale lashing the mountain.

'I wish Erishkigal was here!' Zillah said to Noah.

'Erishkigal? You mean that old woman who smelled like a goat?'

'That was the one, but she was a brilliant midwife.'

'Well, you know what to do.'

'I think so - only this will be my first time.'

Fortunately, however, there were no complications and the baby arrived safely. It was a girl – a healthy-looking scrap with a wisp of black hair and a loud bellow. Zillah wiped her carefully, wrapped her in a shawl and gave her to Shem to hold.

Ishtar looked at him, her eyes brimming with tears. 'I've failed you! I didn't give you a son.'

But he was gazing at his daughter, murmuring, 'She's ours! She's our very own!'

When Noah saw the baby he was overwhelmed with joy, then he cradled her in his arms.

'Holy One, you have been so good to us, so very good to us. You have blessed us and kept your promise.'

Siduri's son Cush arrived two days later, and two days later still Naamah gave birth to her boy, Gomer. The babies took over the home and Noah marvelled how three such tiny people could monopolise everything. Old memories stirred. He wrinkled his nose at long-forgotten smells and learned once more to ignore bouts of crying.

But for all that he remembered, he had seen little of his sons in their early years. There had been women to assist Zillah while he was always out on the estate. Now, despite all the inconvenience, he was entranced, watching for their first smiles, enjoying their gurgles and even when suffering the indignity of having his beard pulled. Better still, Zillah had come back to life, spending hour after hour rocking the babies and even showing Noah some of her old tenderness.

There had been other births too: the first calves had arrived. 'At last!' Siduri exclaimed. 'There'll be cow's milk. How I've missed it!'

They raced to complete the winter sowing before the first blizzard. There was more land this time, since they had cleared the stones from another field. But all of it would be needed. Supplies from the ark were running out and next year they would have to rely on what they could grow here.

30

The next few years were the happiest of Noah's life. He had a new cottage by the lake and left the heavy work to others. But he was always there for the children, watching as they paddled in the lake, mending their broken toys and wiping away tears.

Each afternoon he sat while the little ones crawled over him and the older children listened to his stories. They knew them word for word and corrected him if he missed anything out.

He told them how the Holy One had made the world and about the beautiful lost garden. He recalled the adventures of Adam, Cain, Seth and Enoch, and best of all his own experience in the Great Flood.

Sometimes they visited the ark. The door had rotted away and inside it was open to the sky; the roof and upper floors had been taken away years ago to build houses. Then the ritual began.

He would point with his stick, explaining what each part of the ark used to look like. He finished with the old walkway, still attached precariously to the wall high above their heads.

'We used to stand up there to look out.'

'Can we climb up, Grandpa?'

'No! It's much too dangerous.'

Afterwards he had a doze while the children played at looking after the animals or made the forbidden climb.

But someone was telling the children less pleasant stories. Often young warriors came bursting through the bushes, brandishing sticks and shouting, 'We're the Cainites! We want slaves!' and once Noah chanced upon several little girls stark naked. They were daubing themselves with mud in a credible imitation of the women who had tried to burn down the ark. There was a big row and they were sent to bed without supper.

'I never thought our family would sink to that,' he said to Zillah. 'I just hope they're not meddling in witchcraft. We must sacrifice to the Holy One to ask his forgiveness.'

That was the last time they spoke. They found her dead next morning, and when Noah was called to her bedside she seemed to be asleep. She looked young again, like the beautiful girl he had married so very long ago.

They laid her to rest near the lake, and after piling the earth back they rolled a large stone on her grave to prevent the animals disturbing her. Then Noah gave thanks to the Holy One for her life.

After that he often sat by her grave, regretting the past and wishing for the opportunity to put his arm around her once more.

'Did she ever forgive me for building the ark and bringing her here?' he mused. 'Could I have been more understanding? Should I have spent more time with her?'

But his grieving was interrupted by preparations for a wedding. Japheth's son Gomer had asked permission to marry Ham's daughter Milcah.

'But they're so young,' Noah said to Siduri.

'You weren't any older when you married Zillah!' she laughed.

Noah now had a new hobby: producing grapes. He had found a vine growing wild up a tree and it reminded him of a vineyard Heth had owned, and the excellent drink he produced.

One autumn he planted out his young vines around a trellis that Ham's boy Canaan had made, and soon it became his favourite haunt. In winter he would often slip off to view the rows of dormant plants and trim the odd branch, then in spring sit in the shade of the new leaves. Summer saw him thinning out the fruit clusters, but autumn was his real delight. He had made a shack and camped out there, checking the grapes until they were ready to pick.

'Do you remember the wine they had in the city?' he asked Ham.

'Yes, it tasted marvellous. Are you going to make some?'

'Maybe, well enough to taste anyway – it's a shame to waste the grapes.'

'Yes, but take it easy. It's powerful stuff.'

Next day Ham appeared with a donkey, carrying a huge bowl and an earthenware jar.

Noah filled the bowl with grapes before hitching up his robe and stepping in gingerly. But by the time he had finished treading them out, his clothes were splattered. Then he emptied the juice into the jar.

Next morning there was a yeasty smell and it was foaming out of the top. It tasted sweet and fruity and it took a lot of self-control to leave it until it stopped fermenting. Then he dipped a small cup in and sipped it carefully.

'Ah! This is really good!' And he refilled his cup several times.

The sun was warm and he had not felt so relaxed in years. Feeling sleepy, he retreated into the shack. Soon he was lying flat on his back with his mouth open, snoring. His robe had risen up round his armpits.

'Grandpa! Are you there?'

Canaan had arrived and was worried there was no trace of him. So he put his head inside the shack and for a horrible moment thought Noah was dead. Then he heard snoring.

'So that's what happens when you drink that wine stuff!' he sniggered. 'I'd best get Dad.'

Ham was working nearby. 'Come on, Dad! Grandpa's fast asleep – and he's hardly got any clothes on!'

Ham chuckled when he reached the shack. 'I told him to be careful. What a sight! Showing everything he's got.'

But Japheth was outraged when Ham told him. 'Haven't you any respect for your father?'

'It's his fault. He's got himself drunk and made a fool of himself.'

'But we should cover up for his mistakes.'

'Well, he's not very good at covering himself!'

Japheth went to find Shem and they hurried over to the shack carrying a large robe. Standing outside they arranged it over their shoulders, then backed in, taking care not to look at him. Then they lowered it until he was covered.

'I hope Ham's had the sense to keep his big mouth shut,' Japheth said grimly, 'or he'll make Father a laughing stock.'

31

Noah awoke feeling sick with a headache. But he became furious when Japheth told him what had happened.

'So Canaan saw me like that and didn't do a thing. I'll throttle him when I meet him!'

Japheth interrupted. 'Please, Father, why not sleep on it before doing anything rash?'

'No. I'll have it out with him and his father tonight when we meet at their home for our harvest supper.'

After they had eaten, Noah made his announcement. 'I think you all know what happened today, so I'm calling you to witness that I am cursing Canaan. He will be the lowest of slaves to his brothers.'

Although Ham was trying to say something, he turned to Shem. 'I bless the Holy One, the God of Shem! Let Canaan be Shem's slave.'

Then he looked at Japheth. 'May the Holy One expand Japheth's lands. He will live in Shem's tents and Canaan will be his slave!'

Then Ham shouted in fury.

'That's the thanks I get for helping you all these years! You go and curse my son! Get out of my house, all of you! And take that drunken old fool with you! I never want to set eyes on him again, with or without a robe!'

'Come back with us, Father,' Ishtar suggested. 'We'll look after you.'

For months Noah was in torment, reliving his shame and blaming himself for making that wine. Ham had been his favourite son, the one with drive and energy, but now he had cut himself off, even from his brothers. Japheth had visited him once only to be threatened with a large dog.

Noah was desolate. 'I can't imagine why he shamed me like that. We taught him to respect his elders.'

'He's proud, that's the trouble,' Japheth replied, 'and you humiliated him in front of everyone.'

'As he had humiliated me first. But I still love him and would give anything to get him back.'

'But why did you curse Canaan? Shouldn't it have been Ham?'

'My grandfather Methuselah used to say, "When you judge a man, you judge his father." If I'd condemned Ham, I'd have condemned myself. But in any case I only said what the Holy One gave me. He told me Ham's family would take an inferior place.'

It was the hardest winter ever. Shem had sited his house carefully, facing south and sheltered on the other three sides, but even here the snow piled up in great drifts and for months they only went outside to feed the animals.

By now Noah was blaming himself for what had happened. But then one day Ishtar stopped him.

'I know you thought the world of Ham, but actually he used to laugh about you behind your back. He reckoned you'd gone soft in the head. And who do you think taught the girls to take their clothes off and paint themselves?'

Sadly any chance of a reconciliation ended the next spring with the news that Ham had left, taking his family back to the Great Valley. Then Shem thought of a way to distract his father. 'Why not get your clay tablets out and read them to us?'

This idea proved a great success, cheering Noah up, and prompted a fresh idea. 'Father. You could write some more tablets yourself, telling how you made the ark and what happened in the flood.'

'Of course! That's what I promised Methuselah and Lamech. And I also agreed to teach you to read them.'

'I'm a bit old for that, but why not show my sons?'

Shem's third son, Arphaxad, proved the best pupil. Soon he could read and draw the signs, so Noah dictated his history to him.

After giving some family details, he mentioned the sin of the ancient world and how it had grieved the Holy One. Then he described the ark and the animals, what happened in the flood and the covenant the Holy One gave afterwards.

Then, after many days, Arphaxad laid down his reed pen.

'We've finished, Grandfather.'

'But we haven't mentioned the time I was drunk.'

'Grandfather! But you can't put that in!'

'I'm going to be completely honest and I must say what Ham and Canaan did.'

Shem went to the Great Valley in a last attempt to meet Ham, but he came back discouraged. 'There's violence and immorality everywhere,' he told Noah, 'and they are worshipping the old gods, practising witchcraft and throwing babies into the flames.'

Noah wept. How could his own family turn their back on the Holy One after all he had done for them?

'I've wasted my life!' he cried. 'The world's just as bad as it ever was. We all carry the seeds of wickedness in us, and I with my drunkenness am as bad as everyone else!'

But Ishtar did not agree.

'The Holy One chose you to build the ark because no one else could. Without you, none of us would be alive today. I remember you bursting into my room and carrying me off on your shoulder with hardly a stitch on!'

Noah grinned despite himself.

'I used to believe in a lot of gods, but they never did anything for me. But it was the way you lived that convinced me that the Holy One was the true one, and I know a lot of other people who feel the same.'

That night Noah dreamed he was a boy again, listening to Methuselah. It was the familiar story of Enoch and how he confronted an angry mob telling them that the Holy One would come to judge them with hundreds of thousands of believers.

Then at last he understood. 'Hundreds of thousands – why, that's more than all the people who have ever lived. He must have been talking about another judgement, one which hasn't happened yet, and that also means there are going to be a huge number of believers like Ishtar.'

Then he dreamed he was in a great city, but far better than the one he had known. It shone so brightly it hurt his eyes, but he could see a river lined with great trees bearing flowers and fruit. The streets were made of gold and filled with happy, singing people. They seemed more alive than any he had ever known. Then finally he saw the Holy One with a robe, white as snow, a gold girdle around his chest, and eyes that burned like a furnace. Then their eyes met.

Next morning he felt ecstatic.

'You look happy, Father,' Ishtar said in surprise.

'I saw the Holy One last night, face to face, and he was wonderful. I've been worrying about so many things lately, but now I've met him nothing else matters, nothing at all!'

Note for the reader

The events depicted in *The Oncoming Storm* are based on the stories recorded in Genesis 6–9. The author has woven these stories together with biblical background and evidence of contemporary archaeology to help you explore the difficult questions that the Bible text raises.

Read the Bible passages about Noah and reflect on what they tell you about God. What is God saying to you through these stories? If you have any questions, find a Christian you trust and chat through your ideas, thoughts and concerns.

What are Dark Chapters?

What is the Christian response to the vast array of horror books aimed at young people? Is it to condemn these titles and ban them from our shelves? Is it to ignore this trend and let our young people get on with reading them? At Scripture Union, we believe this presents a fantastic opportunity to help young people get into the pages of God's Word and wrestle with some of the difficult questions of faith.

The text does not sensationalise the horrific aspects of each story for entertainment's sake, trivialising what the story has to say. On the contrary, each retold account uses the more fantastic and gruesome epsiodes of each character's story to grip the reader and draw them into assessing why these events take place.

The reader is asked throughout the books to consider questions about the nature of God, how we should live as Christians, what value we place on things of this world – power, wealth, influence or popularity – and what God values.

Babylon

Daniel is far from home. Jerusalem has been decimated and he has been taken back to Babylon, the most powerful city in the world. As he enters the gates, he feels sick with revulsion. This will be his home for the next seventy years, perhaps even more, but will he be able to stay true to Yahweh, even despite the horrific dangers that will bring?

Babylon

Hannah MacFarlane

£5.99
978 1 84427 618 9

Izevel, Queen of Darkness

Slowly, slowly, slowly, Izevel Princess of Tyre, works her influence over her new husband, Ahav, and his kingdom Israel. Leading them away from Adonai, she encourages the unspeakable practices of Baal worship. But despite her best efforts, the Lord and his prophets will not be disposed of so easily. Increasingly driven mad by her own lifestyle, Izevel races headlong towards her own grisly downfall.

Izevel, Queen of Darkness

Kate Chamberlayne

£5.99
978 1 84427 536 6

Legion

A man rages on a hillside, driven mad by the voices in his head.

A man sits in a dungeon, plagued by doubt and fear.

Both are crushed by their demons. For one, freedom is only moments away, but for the other, it is only the end of his life that is near. Jesus is central to both their lives, but which one will live? And which one is about to face a terrible death?

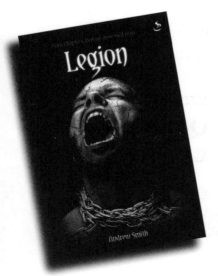

Legion and the Dance of Death

Andrew Smith and Alex Taylor

£1.99
978 1 84427 623 3
£15 for a pack of 20
978 1 84427 629 5

The Egyptian Nightmare

Pharaoh is ruler of all he surveys. His kingdom is prosperous and his monuments are being built at a fantastic rate by his Hebrew slaves. But suddenly, Moses and Aaron appear in his palace and demand the release of the God's people. As events spiral out of his control and God strikes his country with terrifying plagues, Pharaoh's desperate attempts to regain power only lead to his own destruction.

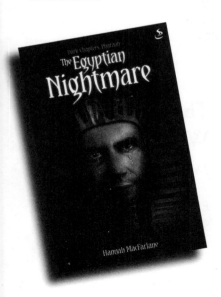

The Egyptian Nightmare

Hannah MacFarlane

£5.99
978 1 84427 535 9

The Sky will Fall

Shimsom thought back over all he had achieved for the Lord. He was one of God's judges, appointed by the Lord to guide his people and rid them of Philistine rule. But Shimsom's methods – a donkey's jawbone, pairs of foxes, a Philistine marriage – had led him here, tied to pillars in the Temple of Dagon. But if he was going to meet a gruesome end, then he would take everyone else with him…

The Sky Will Fall

Darren R Hill

£5.99
978 1 84427 537 3